the Palomino ☆ Pony Comes Home

Look out for:

the
PALOMINO
✿PONY
RIDES
OUT

the
PALOMINO
✿PONY
WINS
THROUGH

the PALOMINO ★ PONY COMES HOME

OLIVIA TUFFIN

nosy crow

With special thanks to Michelle Misra

First published 2014 by Nosy Crow Ltd
The Crow's Nest, 10a Lant Street
London SE1 1QR
www.nosycrow.com

ISBN: 978 0 85763 303 3

A CIP catalogue record for this book is available from the British Library.

Printed and bound in the UK by Clays Ltd, St Ives Plc.
Typeset by Tiger Media Ltd, Bishops Stortford, Hertfordshire

Papers used by Nosy Crow are made from wood grown in
sustainable forests.

5 7 9 8 6 4

www.nosycrow.com

For Pip, Clive and Mossy,
my favourite dog, person and pony!
O.T.

PROLOGUE

"Just move, Lily. Go forward!" The rider's steely-blue eyes flashed angrily as she sat astride the golden palomino pony. She turned back to her mobile, but not before she had given the little mare a hefty kick.

The pony's nostrils flared and she snorted, but still she refused to walk on. Tentatively, she eyed the bushes ahead of her, her ears twitching back and forth.

"ENOUGH!" the girl cried. "Just do as I say!" With a loud thwack, she brought her riding crop down hard on the pony's hindquarters.

CRACK!

The mare wheeled round with a cry of pain that seemed to echo through the depths of the surrounding countryside. Then, just at that moment, a pheasant exploded out in front of them, squawking and flapping. Catching her footing on the hard, frozen tarmac the startled pony slipped, her hooves scrabbling and sparking.

"I said, go on!" the girl cried out. She struck the pony hard on her flanks again, frightening her even more. The mare reared in a moment of blind panic, tossing her head and showing the whites of her eyes.

The girl was thrown off clear into the road, rolling out of the way as the pony slipped on to her side, scrambling and struggling on the muddy ground.

"Jemma … Jemma … are you all right?" A voice crackled through the mobile lying on the road.

As the girl lay winded and bruised, the pony scrabbled to her feet, her saddle slipping to one side and her reins broken.

Desperate to get away from the girl, the pony wheeled round and galloped wildly down the quiet road, veering on to a track that opened out to the moor beyond. With nothing to stop her, the pony raced and raced as if her life depended on it.

When she had covered at least three miles, the palomino finally slowed. She snorted into the clear crisp air, her breath hanging in a silver plume. She was safe at last.

CHAPTER ONE

"Phew, what a day that was!" Georgia slumped into her seat as the dark-green horse lorry pulled out of the showground. It was the first time she'd had a chance to relax all day, she'd been so busy grooming, plaiting and polishing. She hadn't actually ridden herself but she wasn't complaining. She loved being around horses and it was a real treat watching them compete.

Georgia especially loved Wilson, the big bay thoroughbred cross, and there was no doubt about it – he'd definitely been the star of the show! Georgia smiled as she pulled her tangled golden hair back into a ponytail. Wilson was owned by the Haydens – Sophie and her mother, Melanie – and was just one of the ponies that Georgia helped looked after in their yard.

"Thanks again for everything you've done today, Georgia," said Melanie as she drove the horse lorry down the bumpy old track and joined a long queue of horseboxes making their way home. "We couldn't have done it without you, could we, Sophs?" She turned to her daughter.

"Er, what was that?" Sophie looked up from the text she'd been busily composing.

"I said we couldn't have managed without Georgia's help today, could we?" Melanie frowned at her daughter, who was still engrossed in her phone.

"Er, no," Sophie mumbled. She was sitting between her mother and Georgia, a handful of rosettes spread across her lap.

Sophie sounded uninterested but Georgia knew that she wasn't being offhand. She just wasn't passionate about the looking-after part of being around horses, in the way that Georgia was. Sophie was going off to university next year, and at the moment her friends and her social life were probably more important to her than winning at the show.

Sophie finally pocketed her phone and grinned at Georgia. "I bet you'll be glad to see your bed tonight, eh, G?"

"You can say that again!" Georgia laughed. She was tired, but it was the best kind of tired. There was nothing she loved more than being at the

Haydens' yard and watching Sophie ride Wilson. Sophie was seventeen, three years older than Georgia, and she was already an amazing rider. Georgia hoped that one day she'd be as good.

"Well, I think you both did really well today," Melanie grinned. "A great team effort!"

Georgia smiled as she gazed out of the window, passing villages and fields. Today had been magical – the Wadebridge Show: a whole day to totally lose herself in horses. Georgia had wanted it to last for ever – not least because she knew that when she got home, she'd be thrown back into the reality of school and revision. Her end-of-year exams started tomorrow, and she hadn't done nearly enough work for them. "So how long will it take to get back?" she asked Melanie, biting down thoughtfully on her bottom lip.

"Probably a good couple of hours in this traffic," Melanie answered.

Georgia nodded. She'd thought as much. And once they were at the yard she'd have to help Sophie put Wilson to bed, unpack the lorry and do all the general tidying up before she could even think about any revision. Still, it was worth it. Helping out at the Haydens' was the closest that Georgia would get to ever owning her own pony and she relished every moment of it. Money had been tight in the Black household ever since her dad had left years ago and there was no way that her mum could afford the cost of expensive riding lessons, let alone the upkeep of a horse. If it hadn't been for all the riding that Melanie let her do in exchange for helping out at the yard, the only contact Georgia would get with ponies would be in her dreams!

Georgia turned to speak to Sophie, but the older girl's mobile had beeped and she was deep into her texting again.

the
PaLOMiNO ✿PONY

Georgia smiled to herself. Oh, to live in Sophie's world where no matter what, the ponies would always be there...

Chapter Two

Two hours later, and the horse lorry was turning up the drive to the Haydens' house. Redgrove Farm was a large modern building with stables attached, and fields and paddocks that stretched for as far as the eye could see. As the lorry drew to a halt in the yard, a tall, dark-haired man opened the front door.

"So, how did it go?" Simon Hayden asked.

"It was great, Dad," said Sophie, jumping down and pushing past him, nudging him affectionately as she went.

Sophie's dad rolled his eyes and gave Georgia a long-suffering grin as she got out of the horse lorry.

"Hey, hon," Melanie yawned, waving at her husband. Three noisy terriers yapped at her feet. "Get down, boys. Down!"

Georgia stretched – her arms and legs were stiff and aching. It was a lovely warm evening, the heat from the day still hanging in the air.

"Come on, Wilson, easy does it." Melanie soothed the bay gelding as she pulled down the ramp and led him into the yard. "Do you mind taking over, Georgia?" she asked, having glanced around for Sophie.

"Sure," said Georgia, taking the lead rope. "Come on, Wilson."

Once the thoroughbred cross was settled in his stable, Georgia ran over to a nearby barn to fetch a hay net. After giving him a final brush-down and checking he was fed and watered, she turned him out into the field for the night. She took off his head collar and put her arms around his neck, breathing in the gorgeous scent of horse mixed with citronella shampoo. "Off you go, boy," she murmured, patting his hindquarters.

Callie, Sophie's old pony, trotted eagerly over to join Wilson.

"Hello, you," smiled Georgia, giving the mousey dun pony a kiss on her nose.

Callie had been a champion pony in her time but she'd recently been retired. Georgia adored the little Exmoor pony that she'd learned to ride on.

Melanie and Georgia's mum were old friends, and after Lucy Black's husband left, she thought taking her daughter over to Redgrove would be a good distraction. Georgia had immediately loved the ponies and as soon as her mum thought she was old enough, Melanie had started to lead her round the paddock on Callie. And the rest was history! Redgrove had quickly become a home-from-home for Georgia.

"You look very thoughtful." Melanie came up behind Georgia, breaking the spell.

"Oh," Georgia said with a smile. "I was just remembering the first time you put me on Callie."

Melanie patted her on the arm affectionately. "That seems like yesterday!" She smiled warmly. "I can drop you home if you like."

"Really? That would be great, thanks," said Georgia. "You've remembered that I can't come up here after school this coming week, haven't you? Exams."

"Yes, I know," said Melanie. "What will we do without you?"

"You'll manage just fine." Georgia grinned, feeling secretly pleased by Melanie's words.

"When the exams are over you'll have Wilson all to yourself, you know," Melanie continued.

"Really?" Georgia was surprised.

"Yes," said Melanie. "Just for a few days during the first week of the holidays. Sophie's got a job at a local summer camp. So you can exercise him every day if you want to."

"*If* I want to!" cried Georgia, rushing over to give Melanie a massive hug. "I can't wait!"

Melanie smiled. "Simon," she called over her shoulder to her husband. "I'm just going to drop Georgia back." She pulled out the car keys from her pocket and walked over to a shiny new four-by-four that was parked in the yard.

Georgia sighed. Oh, to live like the Haydens.

Not only did they have the most amazing stables for their horses, but their grounds had a swimming pool and a tennis court too. Still, they worked hard for their lifestyle and were very down-to-earth and friendly.

As the four-by-four splattered down the lane, Georgia thought about home. What would her mum be up to at that moment? Probably still painting, as she was busy with an important commission. Georgia's mum was an artist and worked every possible hour to make ends meet. When Georgia had left early that morning for the show, she was up and already absorbed in her latest picture.

The four-by-four turned the corner at the end of the bumpy lane and on to the main road, its headlights lighting up the twilight. After about a mile, they pulled up outside a cottage.

"Thanks, Melanie," said Georgia as she jumped

out of the car. She gave her mum's friend a wave before turning to walk up the path.

The house was quiet when Georgia opened the front door. As she entered the kitchen she could just about hear the faint sound of the radio coming from the shed at the end of the garden where her mother worked.

Dumping her stuff on the kitchen table, Georgia ran over the small lawn. Pip, her faithful black and white spaniel who had been dozing in the last of the evening sunshine, sprang up to greet her, her tail thumping.

"Hi, Mum," she called, poking her head round the door of the shed.

"Oh, hello, sweetheart." Georgia's mother looked up. "I must have lost track of the time." She pushed back a stray piece of hair that had fallen across her face and smoothed her paint-splattered apron. "Have you had a good day?"

"Yes, great, thanks." Georgia bent down to give her mum a kiss. "Have you eaten?"

"Just a sandwich," her mother answered. "I grabbed one earlier. What about you?"

"I had something at the show," said Georgia.

"So? How did they do?" her mum asked.

"Two firsts and three seconds." Georgia grinned.

"Fantastic!" her mum enthused. "But you look shattered, love. It's bed for you now. You need an early night for school tomorrow."

School. Georgia groaned but she knew her mum was right. "OK, Mum," she said.

"Did you get some revision done in the horse lorry like you promised?" her mum asked.

"Yes," Georgia said, crossing her fingers behind her back.

"That's good." Lucy Black nodded as Georgia hurried back to the cottage and up the stairs.

Once Georgia was in her tiny room, where

every surface was decorated with photos and posters of horses or her mum's paintings, exhaustion swept over her. It was no good – she couldn't revise now. She'd have to get up early and do a bit of work in the morning. Trying not to look at the pile of school books stacked precariously on her desk, Georgia put on her pyjamas and sank gratefully into bed.

She fell asleep instantly and was soon dreaming about her favourite thing in the world – ponies! Beautiful bay hunters with smooth paces, little hacks with flowing manes, and flashy showjumpers flying over fences...

CHAPTER THREE

"Georgia!" came her mum's voice the next morning. "Are you ready for school?"

Groaning, Georgia opened one eye and reached out to grab her alarm clock. What time was it? Eight o'clock! There wasn't going to be any time for revision. At this rate, she was going to be late for school!

Gently, Pip licked her cheek as Georgia rolled

over, trying to focus on the day ahead. She only had five minutes to get dressed and grab some breakfast.

Georgia pulled on her navy school uniform, brushed her teeth and tied her hair back before rushing down the stairs.

A smell of sizzling bacon filled the air. Her mum was in the kitchen when Georgia pushed open the door. She looked tired and drawn, and there were dark circles under her eyes.

"You didn't work through the night, did you, Mum?"

"Morning, sweetheart." Georgia's mother grinned, not answering the question, which definitely meant that she had. "All set?"

"As set as I'll ever be," said Georgia, stroking Ralphy, their large tabby cat, and then grabbing a piece of toast. She took a slug of her mum's tea and kissed her on the cheek. "Bye, Mum."

"Take another piece of toast at least!" Lucy Black said. "You need to keep your strength up—"

But Georgia was out of the door. Quickly she ran down the little lane that led to the main road, not stopping until she reached the end. The school bus was already rattling round the corner, with Georgia's best friend, Emma, inside.

"Over here, G." She grinned as Georgia made her way down the aisle. The two of them had been friends since their first day at primary, although they couldn't be more different if they tried – Emma was well-dressed with neat brown hair whereas Georgia was scruffy and her long blonde hair hung down her back in a tangle most of the time.

"I'm so nervous, G," Emma said once Georgia had sat down, her smooth forehead creasing with worry.

"You'll be just fine, Em," said Georgia, giving

her friend a little hug. "You've got nothing to worry about."

As the bus rattled along its route, Georgia starting madly flicking through pages of notes, desperate to cram in some last-minute facts before they arrived at school.

When the bus came to a standstill, Georgia and Emma jumped down and walked up the steps of a red-bricked, modern building. Pupils were jostling for space in the corridors and nervous chatter filled the air.

"See you later, Em," Georgia called over her shoulder as they filed into the exam hall. Quickly, she found her place and sat down. Twiddling her pen anxiously, she stared at her bitten fingernails and then glanced across at Emma.

"Good luck," she whispered before the teacher in charge told them to turn their papers over.

The exam was a disaster. Georgia knew that the minute she saw the questions. As she came out of the room to excited chatter, Georgia felt sick. How had she thought she would be all right? And the exams were only going to get worse with every day that passed.

It was true. As Wednesday became Thursday, and Thursday spilled into Friday, the exams all started to blur for Georgia. She was just relieved when finally they were over. On Friday afternoon, as they emerged from the school building into bright sunshine, relief swept over her.

"Phew! Thank goodness that's over!" Georgia turned to Emma with one thought and one thought only – she had to see the ponies! She hadn't been up to the stables all week and it had nearly killed her!

"Come with me to Redgrove, Em," Georgia begged.

23

Emma rolled her eyes. "I don't know … I want to get home and put together an outfit for the midsummer dance."

"The midsummer dance!" cried Georgia. "But that's ages away. Not till way into the holidays. Can't you think about anything else?"

"It's better than thinking about horses all the time!" Emma teased.

"I don't know if it is," Georgia replied truthfully. "Look, if I come shopping with you on Sunday, will you come up to the yard with me now?"

Emma pretended to look thoughtful for a moment. Then she gave her friend a massive grin. "Done," she said.

The two girls laughed as they ran for the bus.

"Redgrove – here we come!" cried Georgia.

Chapter Four

The yard was quiet that afternoon so it didn't take Georgia and Emma long to race through the jobs that hadn't been done all week. It had been lovely to see the horses, but Georgia was exhausted by the time she got home – and grateful when, finally, she could get into bed. It had been a tiring week.

When Georgia woke the next day, the first thing

that popped into her head was the exams. And then she remembered. They were over! All done! Not only that, but it was Saturday and what with the sun peeking through the curtains, it looked like it would be the perfect day for riding!

Georgia got out of bed and flung back the curtains before throwing on pink shorts and a stripy T-shirt. Next, she packed her navy jodhpurs, brown jodhpur boots and half chaps, and finally put her riding hat in at the top before zipping up her bulging rucksack.

Her mum wasn't awake yet so she tiptoed quietly around downstairs, getting herself breakfast. "Morning, Pip!" she whispered, patting the little spaniel as she stepped out into the sunshine after scribbling her mum a note.

Quickly, she cycled the short journey down the bumpy lane, along the main road and over to the farm.

Melanie was already busy watering her hanging baskets when Georgia propped up her bike by the fence. She waved at her.

"You're here bright and early," she laughed. "Would you mind bringing Wilson in? I was just about to but wanted to get my plants watered before it gets too hot. Sophie's got a lesson over at Janey Meadon's at nine."

"Sure," said Georgia. She liked Sophie's riding instructor. Janey was putting together a showjumping team for the Round Barrow Pony Club and Sophie was one of the four riders who'd been selected. Georgia loved going along to the team practices, hoping she might pick up any snippet of advice. "So where's Sophie?" she asked.

"Still in bed." Melanie rolled her eyes and turned the hose off. "Some party she went to last night … didn't get in till twelve."

"Sounds like fun!" Georgia giggled, fetching

27

Wilson's smart leather head collar and lead rope, though, in all truthfulness, she couldn't think of anything worse. She'd much rather be up early with the horses than out late. She grinned at Melanie and then headed off to the fields to collect the bay.

Once she'd brought Wilson back to the yard, leaving Callie quietly grazing in the fields, Georgia set to work. He was really dusty from rolling on the dry earth, so she brushed him vigorously with the body brush before damping down his shiny black mane with water. Once he was shining all over and she had picked out his hooves and painted them with hoof oil, she stood back to admire her handiwork. "There you go, boy," she murmured contentedly. "All done."

Wilson stood quietly, his eyes half closed, his bottom lip drooping with contentment.

Georgia was just about to put on his bandages

for the short ride in the lorry when Sophie appeared. "Hi," she said unenthusiastically.

She looked tired, with last night's mascara still round her eyes and her hair in a messy bun on top of her head. Her friend, Tory, was with her and she was staring at Georgia with disdain.

Georgia frowned. She didn't like Tory. Sophie and Tory had been friends for years, but Georgia had no idea why – she thought Tory was stuck up and rude. The only good thing about her was her pony, Nightingale!

"Oh, look, Sophie, your little groom is here," Tory said unkindly.

Georgia sighed inwardly. *Here we go again!*

"Tory…" Sophie giggled nervously, looking embarrassed, but that didn't seem to stop the other girl.

"We could have stayed inside a bit longer," Tory went on. "Georgia's in her element out here

29

doing the dirty work."

"Don't be so mean, Tor," Sophie said, eventually, flushing.

Georgia also went red and turned away. She was well aware that she didn't fit in with Sophie's posh school friends, but was there really any need to be so rude?

Tory smirked. "We should get going, Sophie," she said. "Mum's going to meet us at Janey's with Nightingale. Harry's going to be there too." She gave Sophie a knowing little smile and raised an eyebrow.

"Harry?" said Sophie. "Harry Blake?"

"Is there any other Harry?" said Tory, at which point Sophie blushed and giggled.

Honestly! Georgia rolled her eyes. Those two were boy crazy. Georgia couldn't see what all the fuss was about Harry Blake. In fact, she thought he was pretty boring. Still, he did have a lovely horse – a big skewbald gelding called Hector.

"So what do you think Harry will say when…"

The two older girls started gossiping and Georgia busied herself with loading Wilson into the lorry. Once he was secure, she went to look for Melanie.

"Wilson's all done," she said, popping her head round the kitchen door.

"Thanks, Georgia." Melanie gave her a warm smile. "Shall we get going then?"

"Sure." Georgia nodded gratefully, happy to be included on the outing. "I'm ready."

✩ ✩ ✩

Janey Meadon was already waiting for them at her stables when the horse lorry drew up into the yard. Harry was there too, along with another girl whom Georgia recognised as Lottie Fisher. They were the other two members of the Round Barrow showjumping team.

Once they were all mounted and their practice was underway, Georgia watched eagerly as the students trotted and cantered effortlessly around the arena, before neatly jumping the coloured poles and grids that Janey had put up.

"That's it, try and ease him into the double, Sophie," Janey was calling. "In and out."

Georgia was in her element. She loved watching Wilson jump, his kind honest face lighting up at the sight of the fences as he flew over them with ease, never refusing or running out.

"One day I hope I'll be able to do that," she murmured to herself.

When the session came to an end, Janey gestured across to the riders. "Meet me in the tack room. Team talk," she told them.

Georgia went forward to take Wilson's reins from Sophie as she dismounted and began walking him around to cool him off. Wilson barely looked tired but still she concentrated on making sure he was cooled properly before sponging him off and then throwing on his sweat rug. Then she tied him up securely outside the lorry.

The team talk had obviously been brief, as Sophie and Tory were hanging round outside the tack room, chatting with Harry, who was leaning against his horsebox and trying to look all laid back and mature.

Georgia laughed to herself and patted Wilson. "I'd much rather have a pony over a stupid boyfriend any day," she told the horse, who paused from tearing at his hay net to rub his head on her T-shirt, as if in agreement. She felt a bit disappointed at not having had the chance to ride all day, but consoled herself with the thought of the summer holidays just around the corner – and that first week when she'd have the horses all to herself. She couldn't wait. Just one more week of school to get through and that would be it. The whole of the summer holidays lay ahead of her with weeks and weeks of hanging out with ponies to look forward to!

CHAPTER FIVE

It was a couple of days later when Georgia's bubble burst. She was sitting in the head teacher's office with her mum, who had been called in for a meeting, trying to focus on what Mrs Jenkins was saying.

"The exam results weren't good, Georgia." Mrs Jenkins looked up from her desk, peering over half-moon glasses. "I'm worried about you starting your GCSEs on the back of them. You might need to retake this year, you know. "

Georgia began to feel panicky. She definitely didn't want to stay back a year! Out of the corner of her eye she saw her mother frowning.

Mrs Jenkins continued. "But there is another option. You could take a very intensive course in your weakest subjects at a summer school in Wales. We've found in the past that it can get failing pupils back on track in no time."

"Summer school?" Georgia looked at her mother.

"If only you could apply yourself a little better to your work, Georgia," Mrs Jenkins continued. "Your teachers say that you're always daydreaming in class. But you're a bright girl, and it would be a shame for you to resit the year. If you spent a week at this summer school you could brush up on your geography and history, and your grades would be sure to pick up."

Mrs Jenkins turned to Georgia's mother. "Don't worry, Mrs Black. The course is subsidised. There would only be food and accommodation to pay for and that's very reasonable."

Georgia swallowed hard. She felt terrible. Money was tight enough in their house without her mother having to find extra for a course she shouldn't even need to do. She couldn't bear to look up at her mother's expression. She knew it would be anxious and concerned.

Mrs Black cleared her throat. "Mrs Jenkins," she said politely. "When would the course start?"

"Next week," replied Mrs Jenkins. "The first week of the holidays."

Georgia felt hot tears pricking the back of her eyes. It was the week that Melanie had said she could have Wilson all to herself!

"Well, it sounds like a very good idea to me," said Georgia's mum. "You can't afford to fall behind in your schoolwork, Georgia. It's too important."

Georgia groaned inwardly and slumped back on to her chair.

Mrs Jenkins softened a bit. "Come on, Georgia," she said kindly. "It's only a week and they try to make it as fun as possible. There's some written work, of course, but there's a lot of field work too, and Brecon is a lovely part of the world…"

This didn't help Georgia's mood one little bit but she did her best to smile. "OK."

"Super!" Mrs Jenkins beamed. "Well, make sure you take plenty of wet-weather gear, won't you? Unfortunately the forecast is for rain!"

Great, even better, Georgia thought to herself, a lump once again rising in her throat as she thought about how much pony time she was going to be missing out on.

✿ ✿ ✿

And so Georgia found herself on the coach on Monday morning, the rain pouring down outside, heading for some summer school she didn't even want to go to. But she had no choice. She definitely didn't want to stay back a year and be apart from Emma or her other friends, and she had promised Mum that she would try harder at school. Or rather, Mum had spelled it out for her – either she concentrated on her schoolwork more or they would have to rethink how much time Georgia spent at the stables.

Georgia had felt like curling up into a little ball under her duvet. She knew the horses would be waiting for her when she got back, but she'd missed her chance to have Wilson all to herself. Before she left, she had cried and cried for what seemed like for ever into his dark mane.

And now, gazing forlornly out of the window

at the downpour outside, Georgia was finding it hard to be positive. As they crossed a huge bridge over the river and headed into Wales, the sky seemed to darken even more and even heavier raindrops pelted the bus, throwing Georgia into an even blacker mood.

After what seemed like hours, the coach came to a stop at a building in the shadows of a large mountain range and, amid groans, everyone got off into the torrential rain.

They were thrown straight into the course. Within an hour of arriving, they were sent off on a geography field trip to identify as many wild plants as possible. It was supposed to be an ice-breaker – getting them all to work together.

However, Georgia felt as though things couldn't get much worse. Grumbling to herself as she picked her way along the muddy footpath, her negative thoughts were suddenly interrupted by a voice that she vaguely recognised.

"Hey, you're in Emma Clark's class, aren't you?"

Georgia looked back to see a boy with sandy hair, a slightly crooked nose and a smattering of freckles. It was Dan Coleman, a local farmer's son. She didn't know him very well but she knew he was in her year at school.

"Yes, I am." Georgia hesitated. "She's my best friend."

"I like Em." He grinned. "We need a partner for this exercise, so how about it? I'm rubbish at this kind of thing, by the way!"

Georgia laughed. "You're not exactly selling the idea!" she said. "Though I doubt I'll be any better at it than you. The only plants I know are the ones that might be poisonous to horses!"

"Ah," Dan said with a smile. "So you're the girl who's mad about ponies. Can't see the appeal myself; much prefer my cows!" But he was still grinning and Georgia found herself feeling a bit more cheerful.

The exercise was long and tedious, but Georgia tried hard to concentrate. By lunchtime, she and Dan had correctly identified seventeen out of the twenty plants and surprised themselves by getting the highest score. Dan gave Georgia a high-five and she laughed again as they set off with the rest of the group for a walk. The course was turning out to be as boring as she had expected but at least she had a companion to suffer along with her.

Their ramble took them through the hills. After a short spell of rain half an hour earlier, the bracken was glistening in the sunlight and the small mountain streams bubbled and churned over rocks. Georgia had to admit that it was a beautiful setting.

"OK, everyone. I think we've been walking

for long enough," one of the teachers announced finally as they neared a few old farm buildings dotted on the hillside. "Let's have a rest before we begin the next exercise."

Gratefully, Georgia laid out her mac and sank down on to the damp bracken before retrieving her water bottle from her bag.

"Fifteen minutes' break and then we move on. That bracken isn't going to draw itself!" the teacher called out.

Georgia groaned. She was just about to close her eyes and turn her face into the sunshine when suddenly a small movement caught her eye. Was that what she thought it was? A little pony? Out here on the mountainside?

Steadying her gaze, Georgia looked more closely. Sure enough, a small way up the hill, a pony stood in a fenced-off area next to what looked like a deserted cottage.

"I'll see you in five," she said hurriedly to Dan as she got to her feet.

"Where are you going, Georgia? Georgia...?"

But Georgia didn't stop to answer. Quickly, she made her way up towards the pony, taking care to slow down when she was close by so as not to spook it.

Georgia stopped a few metres away, next to a gate, while the pony – a palomino mare – stayed up on the hill, looking down. She was quite possibly the prettiest pony Georgia had ever seen; although she looked flea-bitten she had a golden coat with a small pink snip between her trembling nostrils, and huge amber eyes that didn't leave Georgia's face. Her cream mane swept all the way down her shoulder and her high-set tail reached the ground, but both were dirty and full of tangles and burrs. She had a small, neat head, strong legs and rounded, well-muscled quarters. Despite needing a good groom, she was gorgeous!

Georgia remembered that she had a mint in her pocket so, taking it out, she placed it on the flat of her palm and stretched out her hand.

"Here, girl," she called softly.

For a moment it looked as though the pony was going to walk over and take it. Georgia locked eyes with her. "Come on, my lovely," she breathed.

But then, with a snort and a flick of her tail, the palomino wheeled away and cantered off to the furthest corner of the field.

"Bother," Georgia murmured, gazing after the little mare. She checked her watch. Her time was up too. Fifteen minutes had passed in a flash.

Walking quickly back to the group, thoughts of the palomino pony buzzed around her head. What was she doing out here on such a scrubby bit of land? Why did she look so unkempt and where was her owner? A pony was the last thing that Georgia had expected to see on the field trip and she felt a little rush of excitement flood through her.

"Dan ... Dan!" she cried as she arrived, panting, back at the group. "You'll never guess what I just found."

"Not another piece of gorse?" replied Dan, rolling his eyes.

"No, silly," Georgia laughed, nudging his shoulder. "Come and see for yourself! Quickly!" She dragged him to his feet, and hurried back up the path and over to where the little pony now stood, looking warily at the two of them.

"What's it doing out here?" Dan wondered out loud.

Georgia didn't have time to answer him before one of the teachers appeared on the path, calling up to them. "Come on, you two! It's time

to get going. We need to make some drawings
and then analyse our findings from this morning
back at the centre."

Dan shrugged and turned to Georgia. "Never
mind. We can come back another time. We'd better
go."

Georgia sighed. She knew there was no choice,
but as she stood there, looking at the palomino
pony, she felt completely torn. She couldn't bear
to leave, particularly as she knew they were going
to be stuck inside for the rest of the day having
lessons. Still, she had vowed to Mum that she'd do
her best on this course.

Taking one last look at the pretty mare, Georgia
made another promise. "I'll be back tomorrow,"
she breathed. "You'll see."

CHAPTER SIX

"Cover for me, will you?" Georgia turned to Dan the next day.

They'd had a busy morning's activities on the hillside already, and Georgia had given them her full concentration, but she had been itching to go and check on the palomino the whole time. She couldn't believe she'd had to take pond measurements and dip feeds when there was a beautiful pony so close by! She knew she was breaking her promise to Mum, but the palomino didn't look very well cared for, and she needed to find out more. Mum was a real softie when it came to animals and Georgia knew that in her heart of hearts she'd understand. Well, she hoped she would, anyway. And she could catch up from Dan's notes. So where was the harm? Georgia had texted Melanie last night and told her all about the little mare and Melanie had texted back, sounding intrigued.

"Wait, Georgia… What shall I say?" Dan called out.

But he was too late. Seeing the teacher bent over a map, Georgia had taken her chance and set off, waving over her shoulder and crashing down the hillside. They'd gone further up this morning, but she had made sure that she had her bearings in relation to the cottage on the hill.

She'd even managed to sneak a few carrots from the kitchen when she'd been on washing-up duty that morning.

As quick as she could, Georgia ran down a twisty path, passing little hillocks and mountain streams.

After about five minutes she stopped and looked around her. She could have sworn the pony had been somewhere around here, but now that she had stopped there was nothing in sight that she recognised. Georgia was just about to give up and go back when she heard a faint sound in the distance. It was the quietest of noises, but one that Georgia recognised in an instant – a whinny!

Spinning round, she hurried along the path to her left until she was out on open moorland. And there in front of her was the ramshackle cottage and fenced-off bit of grassland.

"So here you are," she murmured as the little

50

pony lifted her head and stared at her. Someone had clearly been to visit overnight as there was a net of hay tied to the fence and a clean pail of water, but the mare was still as dirty as ever. Georgia longed to give her a good brush, if only she could get close enough.

Tentatively, she made her way over, stopping at the side of the fence.

The pony stood her distance, her nostrils flaring, her head tossing as she eyed the newcomer.

"It's OK, girl," Georgia breathed. "I'm not going to hurt you. I want to be your friend." She pulled out one of the carrots from her pocket and placed it on her hand.

For a moment, Georgia thought that the palomino was going to stay still but, as she stood watching, the pony started to amble forward.

"That's it," Georgia breathed. "Easy does it."

But then, a few of metres short of her, the little

mare stopped in her tracks. "Come on," Georgia coaxed again.

But that, it seemed, was far as the pony's journey would take her.

Georgia coaxed and cajoled for the next twenty minutes or so but still the pony wouldn't budge and Georgia knew she had to admit defeat. She couldn't expect Dan to cover for her for much longer and she'd already been gone half an hour.

Leaving her bundle of carrots on the pony's side of the fence, she reluctantly turned to go. As she made her way back along the path she glanced back one last time at the palomino.

Now Georgia was at a safe distance, the little pony dipped her head down to the pile of carrots and started to munch.

Georgia smiled to herself. "There. That wasn't so bad now, was it?"

CHAPTER SEVEN

For the next couple of mornings, Georgia woke early to go back and see the palomino again. She just couldn't help herself. In fact, in between lessons and fieldwork, the little pony was all she'd been able to think about.

She still hadn't been able to get close to the mare, but on the second morning, as Georgia walked along the path to the cottage, the little pony whickered. It was as though she had been expecting her!

Georgia's heart leapt. "Hello, girl," she responded, reaching out her hand as she leaned over the wooden fencing. The palomino was only centimetres away but every part of her seemed to be on springs, as if she was ready to whirl round and flee.

Carefully Georgia leaned in closer and stretched out a hand.

The pony started immediately, snorting and taking a step back. But then a strange thing happened. She extended her neck, briefly touching Georgia's palm with her nose. Instantly Georgia felt a warm feeling flood through her and her whole body relaxed.

"Well, well, well." A voice came from behind, making Georgia jump.

The noise broke the moment and the pony spun

round and galloped off, spraying Georgia with a fine mist of mud and water. But it had been enough. Georgia had felt something really special. There had been a connection.

Georgia turned to see an elderly man wearing patched tweeds. He was weather-beaten and looked very frail. "So I see you've met Lily," he said finally.

"Lily," Georgia breathed. So that was the name of the mysterious little pony. It was perfect for her.

"You're the first person to get near to her in quite some time," the old man commented. "Apart from me, that is." His accent was strong and lilting.

"I thought I must have done something wrong," said Georgia, smiling, "for it to take so long to make friends with her."

"No, nothing wrong," said the old man. "She's

just very wary. She's had a lot to deal with. But I'm forgetting my manners. Let me introduce myself." The old man held out his hand. "I'm Eric."

"And, um, I'm Georgia," said Georgia, reaching out to shake his hand. "I'm on a field trip just up the road."

"Ah, I thought you weren't from round here," said Eric. "So you like ponies, do you?"

"Like them? I LOVE them." Georgia reddened. "So, do you own Lily? Why is she like this?" She had so many questions.

"Yes, I suppose I own her," the old man said enigmatically. "I've only just got out of hospital," he went on, letting out a heavy cough.

Georgia nodded. It did, at least, explain why the pony hadn't been groomed, although not why she was in such a nervy state. And who had been feeding her?

The old man held out his hand to the little pony and as Georgia watched, Lily walked forward and cradled her head into it. Eric gently stroked her neck.

"I bred her myself," Eric explained. He leaned over the fence and blew into the little pony's nostrils. "She should have been a champion show pony."

The palomino had visibly relaxed and the two of them stood contentedly for quite some time before the old man took a step back.

"Should have been?" Georgia said finally.

"Yes," Eric said. "She came from one of my best mares. But then she was given to Jemma, my granddaughter, and, well, let's just say the rest is history. That was the end of her career."

"Why?" Georgia stared at him. "What happened?"

"An accident," the old man snorted. "Though

it wasn't Lily's fault."

As Georgia gazed at the pretty little pony with her small neat head and her gorgeous liquid amber eyes, she knew it couldn't have been anything she'd done.

"So what happened?" Georgia persisted. She wanted to know everything about the palomino.

"She threw Jemma off." Eric snorted. "Jemma was on her mobile at the time, wouldn't you know it? She tried to push Lily into going forward when Lily wasn't sure. Lily's always been quite a nervy, delicate pony, but she's not a bad'un. That's just part of her make-up. Lily got spooked and ran off. I found her out on the mountainside. My daughter-in-law, Jemma's mother, wanted to have her put down but I wouldn't hear of it. I brought her out here to live with me. It's where I've been since I left the stud farm." He pointed in the general direction of a farm in the distance. "Carlamu," he breathed.

"Carlamu?" Georgia rolled the word over her tongue.

"Yes, the Carlamu Show Stud," Eric explained. "It means 'gallop' in Welsh. I used to own it – but it's my son and daughter-in-law's now. I had to hand over control of the business when I got ill." Eric coughed before continuing with his story. "I'm weary to my bones." He held out his hand and Lily snuffled lightly over it, nudging him affectionately. "That's why she's got to go. I'll miss her when she's gone."

"Gone?" said Georgia.

"Yes," said the old man. "Tomorrow afternoon at four. Jemma and her cousins are coming to collect her. She's going to be sold at the Builth sales on Saturday. I can't take care of her any more."

The man looked upset, shaking his head sadly.

Georgia felt panicked. The sales? That would mean she might never see the little pony again! She couldn't let it happen! In that moment when they had made a connection, Georgia had seen the pony's true spirit and the palomino had stolen her heart.

She bit down hard on her bottom lip. The little pony could be sold to just anybody – a meat man even – the condition she was in! Georgia couldn't bear it.

"Please," she said. "Please, don't let them take her. Please look after her here."

"I wish I could," the old man said, his blue eyes sad and watery. "But there's nothing I can do. I'm not strong enough. It's not what I want for her. I won't be here tomorrow to say goodbye to her. I hate goodbyes." He smiled weakly. "Now, young lady, it was nice to meet you. Enjoy the

rest of your trip."

And with that he turned and limped back down the track, leaving Georgia standing next to the paddock on her own, lost in thought…

CHAPTER EIGHT

Georgia stood quite still, watching the old man go, his walking stick acting as a crutch as he gently propelled himself forward. She felt a lump rise in her throat.

Suddenly there was a noise behind her and a shout. Dan!

"Georgia! Come on!" he called. "You said you'd only be ten minutes. We've got to get back!"

"Get back?" Georgia stared wildly around her, all thoughts of lessons completely forgotten. She couldn't bear to leave Lily to her fate. She had to do something. "Dan, it's Lily," she cried. "I ... er... We need to make a plan!"

"Lily?" Dan looked puzzled.

"The pony," said Georgia impatiently, gesturing at the little mare in front of her. "She's going to the sales at the weekend!" Georgia briefly filled him in on everything that the old man had told her – how Lily had been bred to be a star, how she had been mistreated, before finally finishing on how the palomino was going to be collected the very next afternoon.

Dan was wide-eyed by the end of it. "So what can we do?"

"I don't know!" Georgia wailed. "I need to go back to the centre and think!"

"OK," said Dan. "I'll help you. I'm good at

plans. Although I have to say, I haven't got a clue what we can do about this one!"

Georgia nodded in agreement. She wasn't sure what she was going to do yet either but Dan, with his sensible head and understanding of animals, was a good person to have for help.

Saying their goodbyes to Lily, they headed down the slope and back to the clearing, where the group had been busy doing some more fieldwork. Immediately, the two of them ran into a teacher.

"Miss ... Miss," Dan started, thinking on his feet. "Georgia's feeling dizzy. Can I take her back to the centre?"

"Oh, Georgia, are you OK?" The teacher looked concerned and reached out a hand to feel her brow. "You do seem a bit warm." She hesitated. "OK, go on then. You'd better have a lie down. And perhaps it would be best if you kept an eye on her, Dan, if she's feeling dizzy."

Dan shot Georgia a look and the pair of them hurried away triumphantly.

Once back at the centre, Georgia grabbed her mobile from her overhead locker and hurriedly scrolled through her contacts for Melanie.

"Come on, Melanie … please be there," she murmured as she punched the call button.

Almost immediately there was a familiar voice at the other end. "Hello, Georgia! This is a nice surprise!"

"Oh, Melanie!" Georgia felt so relieved that she started to sob. "It's the pony. The one I texted you about – she's going to be collected for the sales tomorrow." The words tumbled out one after the other. "And I'm so worried that because she's not in very good condition, she'll probably go for meat! But, Melanie, she's such a special pony. You should see her—"

"OK, calm down a minute, Georgia," Melanie

soothed her, from the other end of the line. "Slow down."

"Can you come and see her? Please? There's something about her…"

She heard Melanie take a deep breath.

"OK, listen to me, Georgia," Melanie said. "When did you say she was being sold?"

"Saturday," Georgia replied. "Only she's being collected tomorrow afternoon."

There was a silence at the end of the phone. Melanie was clearly thinking. The seconds seemed like hours. Time hanging in the air as delicate as a spider's web. Lily's life hanging in the balance.

Finally Melanie spoke. "OK, here's the plan," she said. "Simon always tells me I'm reckless and that I follow my heart too much, but you've helped me so much in the past. Look, I'm going to come and see what I can do. I trust your instincts – you have an eye for a good horse – and I'd love to have a palomino at Redgrove. But if I don't think she's right, you'll have to accept that she could be sold."

Georgia took a sharp intake of breath. She could hardly believe what she was hearing.

"I'll drive the lorry down tomorrow morning," Melanie was saying now. "So I should be with you mid-afternoon. Would it be possible for you to go and sit with the pony? So you can explain if someone comes to take her away before I get there. When does your course wrap up?"

"Um," Georgia said hesitantly, thinking fast. "I think we finish around lunchtime and then have a free afternoon. I'll go and watch Lily as soon as I can."

"Great. I'll ring you tomorrow when I'm nearly there," Melanie said. "I'll give your mum a call now and let her know what's going on."

"Thank you, thank you so much," said Georgia. "I don't know what to say."

There was a silence at the end of the phone before Melanie spoke again. She took a deep breath. "Don't thank me – yet…"

"Wow!" Dan said when finally Georgia ended the call and told him what Melanie had said. "Wow, wow, wow! We're going to save her!"

"We certainly are!" grinned Georgia.

And without thinking, Georgia flung her arms around him and gave him the most massive hug, sheepishly drawing back with embarrassment as she realised just what she had done. But she couldn't help herself. There was a real chance that they were going to rescue the gorgeous palomino – and she was over the moon!

CHAPTER NINE

It was quiet on the mountainside the next afternoon as Dan and Georgia sat on a grassy tussock overlooking Lily's field, quietly waiting. No one was about as the sun valiantly tried to make an appearance through the black clouds. Georgia had been right about having the afternoon off, which meant that they hadn't even had to miss any lessons.

Lily seemed to appreciate their company and stood quietly just a few metres away, dozing but with one eye watching them all the time. Dan stretched his long legs.

"Honestly, Georgia, you and your ponies! I'll never understand it!" But he was smiling as he said it.

"What do you mean? They're the most beautiful, most loyal creatures on earth," Georgia said determinedly.

Dan laughed at how earnest she sounded. "I'd quite like to learn to ride myself, you know," he said. "My mum used to have a horse before she died so it would be nice to have that connection with her."

Georgia gasped. "Oh, Dan, I'm so sorry. I didn't know."

Dan shook his head sadly. "Don't worry," he said. "We're OK. Me and my brother, Ben, and

Dad. We manage all right on the farm."

Georgia didn't know what to say. All week she'd been feeling so sorry for herself, and here was Dan having lost his mother. She picked up his hand and then dropped it again, feeling embarrassed.

"Listen!" Dan said suddenly, as voices came drifting over the still air. Just then three figures appeared at the brow of the hill, a teenage girl and two older boys.

The girl was dressed in expensive riding gear and she held a riding crop in her hand. Her blonde hair was cut in a fashionable style and Georgia guessed she was about fourteen. She had a haughty look about her, as if she meant business. It had to be Jemma – Eric's granddaughter.

The two boys were probably a few years older and were wearing weather gear and carrying ropes and, much to Georgia's amazement, what looked like a piece of lead pipe.

"So you're the one who's been hanging around *my* pony, are you?" the girl said, sneering at Georgia as she drew near. "Granddad said something about someone making friends with Lily. Well, thanks for that." Her voice was full of sarcasm. "But you can clear off now." Jemma indicated with her thumb for them to leave. "We need to catch Lily to get her to the sale."

"That's what I wanted to talk to you about," Georgia said firmly, clenching and unclenching her fists, her whole body shaking.

"Oh?" The girl trained her ice-blue eyes on Georgia.

"Yes, er, actually. We would like to buy her, er, before she goes..." The words tumbled out one after the other.

"You?" Jemma laughed, looking her up and down.

"Yes," Georgia stumbled over her words. "Well,

72

no, not me, it's a friend. She's on her way with a horse lorry now."

"Is she now?" The girl laughed again, a cruel mocking sound. "But I don't want to sell her privately. I want her to go for auction – see what I can get for her. With her breeding she'll attract the biggest buyers."

"Oh." Georgia hesitated. Lily was in such a terrible state that she hadn't expected that, but then she had been bred as a show pony, hadn't she? Maybe she would still be worth a lot after all. "I guess we'll just have to go to the sales then," she said, suddenly unsure of herself.

"Fine," Jemma said curtly. "Although you don't look like you could afford a hamster, let alone a pony!"

"Hey, that's enough!" Dan stepped in, but the girl wasn't really listening. She marched towards Lily, who cowered at the sight of her. Just as she got close Lily gave a squeal of fear and galloped off, her ears pinned flat to her head.

"That stupid animal," one of the boys growled. "I knew we should have left her. Right, Andy, go and get the truck. We're going to have to herd her in."

Georgia looked at Jemma, who was red with anger, cracking her crop against her leg.

Lily was trembling now, her pink nostrils flared, blowing hard.

Georgia and Dan watched as the truck was backed into the gateway. Dan had to hold Georgia back as she tried to run forward. "She's not our pony, remember," he said under his breath.

The three of them started to herd the pony towards the truck, one of the boys cracking the pipe at Lily's back legs as she tried to escape.

"No!" cried Georgia, rushing forward, breaking out of Dan's grasp. "Don't hurt her!"

But it was too late. Jemma smacked Lily hard across the haunches with her crop. Lily squealed in pain and reared skyward, knocking Jemma to the ground. Quick as a flash, Jemma jumped up and with a howl of rage she grabbed the pipe the boy was holding.

"Right, you witch," she screamed. "See if you like this!" She raised the pipe as if to strike Lily on the head, but instinctively the palomino wheeled round. Before Georgia knew what was happening, Lily had made a run for it, clearing the sheep hurdle propped against the trailer and escaping the field.

Catching her footing on landing, she stumbled, falling heavily on to her side.

Georgia ran towards her, as did Dan. Lily tried to get up, but she was clearly winded.

"Quick," bellowed Jemma. "Get a halter on her. NOW!"

At the sound of Jemma's voice, the little pony struggled to her feet and galloped blindly off up the hillside. Before anyone could stop her, she was free – running as far away as the eye could see.

Chapter Ten

"This is all your fault!" Jemma turned on Georgia, who was sobbing now. Dan steadied her arm. "Leave the pony," she said to the two boys. "She would have only gone for meat anyway. She's evil and vicious."

"No, she's not," sobbed Georgia. "*You* are. You're the evil and vicious one! She could injure herself at that pace."

Jemma laughed. "Well, let's hope she does."

And with that, Jemma and the two boys clambered into the truck, pulling away fast, leaving great welts in the damp ground.

"What can we do?" Georgia cried out. "We can't just leave. Lily was clearly frightened and she could be hurt. We have to go after her!"

"OK," Dan said hesitantly. "But look, why don't you call Melanie first? See where she is."

"OK." Georgia pulled out her phone and pressed a button. "She must still be driving, Dan," she said when there was no answer. "Come on, let's go."

The two of them broke into a run, following the trail of hoof marks. They ran around the side of the hill and down into a wooded valley. The ground became boggier, with large tussocks that they had to scramble over, but soon they were in the woods, and there were still clear hoof marks in the ground.

After they had been following them for about a quarter of an hour, Dan held up his hand, panting. "Georgia, I'm out of breath. Let's just have a five-minute rest, OK?"

"OK," she agreed, leaning heavily against the nearest tree. Her lungs were on fire and her heart was hammering in her chest. Georgia doubted she could have gone much further either.

The rain started then – big, fat droplets that fell slowly at first. Then the sky opened completely, quickly soaking Georgia and Dan through. Georgia's thin trousers clung to her legs and her hair was plastered against her head, rivulets of water running into her eyes. She started to cry silently. This was hopeless! Lily could be lost in the mountains or, even worse, she could have been run over on the main road. The thought of the beautiful palomino pony being hit by a car twisted Georgia's heart with fear.

Just then Dan touched her on the arm, a finger to his lips. "I heard something," he whispered urgently. "Come on, down towards the river!"

They ran as fast as they could without losing their footing, down to the edge of the bank that dropped steeply to a torrent of water swirling far below. Georgia gave a gasp of horror. She could see a pony. It was Lily! She was trying to cross the river! The water was already up to her hocks, and she was hesitantly trying to edge into the deeper water.

Georgia flung herself down the bank, sliding partway and cutting her hands. Dan was close behind her. Lily gave a start and panicked. Before Georgia had a chance to stop her, the pony had launched herself into the water, paddling furiously against the current.

Dan put a hand on Georgia's shoulder. "She might be able to cross by herself, Georgia. And look, it's fenced the other side, so if she makes it, she won't be able to go any further."

Georgia watched in silent anguish, willing the little pony to get over safely.

"Look – we can get over there." Dan indicated a fallen tree trunk a little further up that spanned a narrow part of the river.

Without further ado, Georgia scrambled along the bank to the trunk and tentatively edged her way across it, not taking her eyes off the palomino. Once Dan was safely across, the two of them raced along the bank so they were adjacent to Lily, who was about two thirds of the way across now, her nostrils flaring with the effort and her eyes huge with fear.

"Come on, Lily," Georgia cried, willing her on. "You can do it!"

But at that moment the pony suddenly disappeared from view, losing her footing in the strong current. Georgia gave a cry of terror.

Then Lily resurfaced, trying frantically to paddle against the strong wall of water, but she was growing weaker, drifting now, as she was pulled along.

Georgia and Dan ran alongside her as she was pulled downstream until they reached another narrow section of water. Georgia immediately began throwing off her mac and shoes.

"What are you doing?" Dan yelled.

"I'm going in!" Georgia replied, sliding down the bank to the cold water.

"No, you don't," Dan replied. "I'm the stronger one!"

And before Georgia could stop him, he had waded in until he was chest deep.

Lily had stopped drifting now and was struggling to the bank, but then she collapsed in the shallower water. Dan reached her quickly, his strong body fighting against the current. Lily was too exhausted to panic as he grabbed her mane, forcing her to keep her head above water. Urging her with every bit of strength that he had, he dragged her towards the bank.

Just then, Georgia heard her mobile ring. Quickly she made a grab for it, but her hands were freezing cold and as she pressed the receive button, she dropped it.

"I'm nearly there!" the phone crackled. It was Melanie on speakerphone. "I'm following your directions. I'm on the main road out of Brecon."

Georgia reached for the mobile again, trembling as she put it to her ear. "You've got to get here quick!" She looked around her, trying to take in the unfamiliar surroundings. "It's the pony! She's stuck. She's in the river!" Georgia could make out the faint hum of the traffic on the road above and hoped it was the route Melanie was taking. "I don't know where we are," she sobbed. "Somewhere below the main road, in some woods." She looked frantically around for landmarks. "There's a sort of barn with a metal roof to the left of me. Please hurry!" she added.

"All right, Georgia, I'm coming. Just be very careful!" As Georgia snapped her phone shut, she heard Melanie putting her foot on the accelerator.

Just then Dan called out, his voice panicked. "Georgia, Georgia, come quickly. I can't hold her any longer!"

Without a second's hesitation, Georgia plunged into the water. Although she could touch the stony bottom of the river bed, the current was strong and the shock of the icy water made her gasp. Her clothes clung heavily to her frame as she struggled across, half swimming, half wading, coughing as the water swirled around her face.

Reaching Dan, she put her arms around Lily's

84

neck, steadying her as Dan once again tried to pull the pony out.

At last, Lily seemed to realise that Georgia and Dan were helping her and stopped fighting against them. She flailed in the shallows before lurching to her feet and clambering towards to the bank. Once she was only fetlock-deep, she stood with her head low and her sides heaving. Her beautiful mane and tail were bedraggled and soaked, and her breath was coming in loud gasps.

Georgia and Dan pulled themselves up the bank before collapsing on the damp mossy ground next to the pony.

CHAPTER ELEVEN

"Georgia! Georgia, where are you?"

After what seemed like ages, Georgia heard Melanie's voice in the distance. "Over here!" Georgia yelled back, her heart leaping. "We're over here!"

And then Melanie was scrambling down the riverbank towards them. She was clutching a head collar in one hand and within moments of arriving had caught Lily, who was too weak to run away again. Keen to get her warm and dry, Melanie carefully led the mare up to the main road where she had parked the lorry.

Melanie's appearance had given Georgia renewed energy and, grasping Dan's hand to steady herself, the two of them slowly made their way up to the road. The sight of the Haydens' familiar horse lorry felt like the best thing Georgia had ever seen, and even more so when Melanie produced three woollen rugs.

She rugged Lily, then passed blankets over to Georgia and Dan, who gratefully wrapped themselves up. "OK, so what's been going on here?" she asked as she looked Lily over, carefully checking each leg for cuts.

Quickly, Georgia explained everything that had happened – about Jemma turning up, and the heated exchange, before finishing on how Jemma had gone to hurt the little pony and how that had made Lily run off.

"Phew, that's quite a story," said Melanie, shaking her head. "Lily seems OK now, but we'll have to get her to a vet to be checked out."

"But what about Jemma? What about buying her?" said Georgia. "If we just take her, isn't that stealing?" The words spilled out.

"We'll sort out buying her once the vet has looked at her and Lily's settled," Melanie said firmly. "For now, what's important is this pony's safety, and that you two get warm and dry. Come on, try not to worry. Everything will be fine. But we need to move fast now."

"Thanks, Melanie," Georgia said gratefully, relieved that an adult was taking control of the situation.

Once Lily was safely loaded and settled in the horse lorry, the three of them climbed in and Melanie turned on the engine.

Just then reality hit Georgia. "School!" she gasped, horrified.

Dan gulped. "Do you think they'll have discovered we've gone?"

"Hmm," said Melanie, wrinkling her forehead as she thought. "Call your parents now and see if they mind if you come home with me early – you were going home on the coach tomorrow morning anyway, weren't you? Then we'll swing by the centre, pick up your bags and explain. Can't see it being a problem, can you?"

Dan and Georgia gazed at her in wonder. Georgia couldn't imagine anyone ever saying no to Melanie, but she wondered what her mum was going to say about her having got herself involved with a pony rescue when she was supposed to be concentrating on schoolwork. She shook the thoughts from her head. She wouldn't have done things differently even if she could have, and she would just have to make it up to Mum and show her that she was going to keep her promise and work hard next term.

"As for Lily," Melanie continued, her smile vanishing. "How are we going to trace this Jemma who owns her? Hmm." She looked thoughtful. "I know – when I'm home, perhaps I can ring the sales. They should have the pony listed in the catalogue, so we'll be able to narrow it down to the ponies who haven't shown."

"Thanks, Melanie," Georgia smiled. "You won't let Jemma take her though, will you? She was so cruel."

"No chance." Melanie turned to Georgia and smiled. "Lily's not going anywhere, not after what you told me about how she was being treated. Don't you worry!"

They stopped at the summer school to explain and to change into dry clothes and gather their things. Then they pulled in at a service station on the motorway on the way home for some reviving hot chocolate.

When they went to check on Lily, they found her standing quietly in the back of the horse lorry. Georgia gently reached out to stroke her muzzle and although the pony flinched, she didn't pull back. Georgia was able to run her hand down the palomino's cheek, still slightly damp from her river adventure.

Melanie looked through the cab door. "She's definitely a beauty," she said. "In spite of the grime and dirt."

Luckily the motorway was quiet as they got underway again and a few hours later the horse lorry was pulling into the drive of Redgrove Farm.

Sophie came out to greet them, a look of curiosity

91

on her face. To Georgia's relief there was no sign of Tory.

As they pulled down the ramp, Lily gave a startled whinny. Georgia approached her slowly and led her out, taking her to a stable where she filled up the water buckets and fluffed up the deep straw bed.

"I've called the vet," said Melanie, poking her head over the stable door a few minutes later. "He's coming round to check her over in the next half an hour."

"Thank you," Georgia said. "Please can I sit with her, just so she's not frightened?"

Melanie smiled. "Of course, but take care. Remember she's nervous so she may do something unexpected."

"Sure," Georgia said quietly. Wilson and Callie had come in for the night, so Lily wasn't in the yard alone. They stood staring in fascination at the new arrival.

Dan yawned. "You know, I think I'm going to get home now," he said. "I need a hot bath."

"Of course," said Georgia. "I can't ever thank you enough, Dan." She stood up and smiled at her new friend.

"OK, well, see you tomorrow?" said Dan, looking a bit embarrassed. "Maybe I could stop in after I've seen to the cows?"

"That'd be great," Georgia said, grinning from ear to ear. "You saved Lily's life. I'm sure she'll be pleased to see you." She put her head down and murmured the rest into Lily's mane. "And I'd love it too…"

As she waved Dan off, a battered old Land Rover turned into the yard and a tall, wiry man got out. The vet had arrived.

"Hi there," he said as he unbolted the stable door. "So who do we have here?"

"Lily. She's very nervous," Georgia explained.

"She certainly is, isn't she?" he said, running his hands down Lily's legs and listening to her heart before finally taking her temperature. Lily trembled violently, but she didn't resist. She obviously sensed that the vet's intentions were good.

"She's fine, but you'll need to keep an eye on her tonight after the shock she's had today," the vet advised. "I'll come out tomorrow and check on her again." He smiled at Georgia, who was still wrapped in the pony rug. "You look exhausted. If I were you I'd go to bed too. Have a warm bath and an early night."

Georgia started to protest but Melanie, who had appeared behind him, agreed. "Come on, Georgia. You must look after yourself. And your mum is desperate to see you."

"All right." Georgia sighed. "As long as I can

come back first thing in the morning."

"Of course you can," said Melanie. "And in the meantime, we'll take good care of her."

✧ ✧ ✧

Georgia let out a deep breath as she submerged herself in the bath. Luckily, once her mother had heard all about the little pony and why Georgia had felt compelled to save her, she had understood. Although she was still concerned about Georgia's schoolwork, she could not bear to hear about an animal being mistreated.

Georgia had never been so grateful to have a hot bath. She must have lain in the hot water for at least an hour, revelling in being warm and clean again. She washed her hair and was just drying it, wrapped up in her fluffy dressing gown, when her mother called up the stairs, sounding anxious. "Georgia, Melanie's on the phone."

Quickly Georgia bounded down the stairs and

grabbed the receiver. After a few moments of listening she spoke firmly. "OK, I'll be right there."

Her mum looked at her as she put down the phone. "Georgia, you are not going out again at this time of night! You need to go to bed."

"But it's Lily!" Georgia wailed. "She's sick! Melanie's had to call the vet back! Oh, Mum, I *have* to see her!"

Chapter Twelve

After persuading her mum to let her go, Georgia pulled on some clothes and sprinted out of the cottage, grabbing her bike. Quickly, she cycled down the roads and up the lane until she arrived at the yard. There she found Melanie leading Lily round. Lily's sides were slick with sweat.

"She's colicking, Georgia." Melanie sounded worried. "I didn't want to call you after the day you've had but I thought you'd want to know. The vet should be back any minute."

Georgia's whole body felt cold. She knew that colic, although fairly common in horses, could be fatal in some cases. Not this, not after everything that Lily had already been through!

"She must have swallowed some river water," said Melanie. "Or perhaps it's delayed shock. Carry on leading her round. I'm going to see where he is. Don't let her roll, whatever you do."

Georgia took the lead rope that Melanie offered and continued to walk Lily round. The little pony's tummy gave an ominous rumble. She was obviously in serious pain and kept trying to paw at her stomach. She looked at Georgia with enormous frightened eyes and began to sink to her knees.

"No!" Georgia begged the palomino, pulling on her with all her strength. She was afraid that Lily was trying to roll, which was the most dangerous thing that a horse with colic could do.

"Please, Lily. Don't give up!" Georgia sobbed, pushing against her shoulder and nudging her to continue around the yard. Just when she thought her legs were going to buckle, the vet appeared, running through the wrought-iron gates. Taking one look at Lily, he snapped open his briefcase and produced a syringe.

"Keep her moving!" he instructed as he measured up a dose of painkillers.

After quickly administering the drug, the vet grabbed the lead rope and took over from Georgia. Lily's eyes were wild now, her ears pinned back with pain and fear. Georgia felt a sob rising in her throat, choking her. The vet was much stronger and managed to keep the little pony walking and, after what seemed like a lifetime, Lily started to calm.

"I'm going to give her some charcoal to soak up whatever's still lurking in her tummy," he explained to Georgia as he listened to Lily's stomach with his stethoscope. "I think she's going to be OK. Luckily Melanie noticed in time before she could roll and twist her guts."

Relief flooded through Georgia.

"She's not completely out of the woods," the vet warned, "but she's a strong pony, and young and fit. Now, put her back in her stable and I'll get going."

✩ ✩ ✩

One long hour later, Lily was starting to show some signs of improvement. Georgia kept her warm with a wool rug. Although it was the middle of summer, the night still had a slight chill and Lily had been sweating heavily. Melanie raked over the floor as Georgia stroked Lily's golden neck, gazing at her white eyelashes and tiny ears.

"You're so perfect," she whispered, and the pony made a quiet nickering sound.

"She's been through a rough time, the poor girl," said Melanie as she filled up Lily's water bucket.

"Let me stay with her tonight!" Georgia begged. "I can keep an eye on her!" She looked at Melanie pleadingly.

Melanie hesitated. "I'm not sure about that, Georgia. We'd need to see what your mother thinks."

"OK, but if she agrees, will you let me?" Georgia persevered.

"OK." Melanie smiled. "Let me phone her now. I guess I could leave the house unlocked in case you needed me."

Quietly, Melanie closed the half-door behind her and made her way over to the house to make the call. She returned a few moments later, carrying a dark-blue blanket. "I've spoken to your mum," she said. "She's not best pleased about it but she eventually said yes."

"That's great!" Georgia grinned through a strand of hair.

"On one condition," said Melanie. "That you eat all of your supper. She's on her way up with it now."

"I think I might manage that," said Georgia. It had been the last thing on her mind, but now that she came to think about it, she was actually feeling rather hungry.

"I'm sure Lily will be very grateful to have you here," said Melanie. "But remember, you must let me know if you need me to take over. Just shout if you need me."

"Thanks, Melanie, I will," said Georgia, settling back down into the straw.

When Georgia's mother appeared ten minutes later, she was carrying a flask of soup, a crusty roll and some home-made cake.

Cautiously, she pulled back the door to the stable. "She's an angel," she breathed quietly as she stood in the doorway.

"I know, Mum," Georgia said proudly. "She's beautiful, isn't she? There's something so special about her. I just love her already!"

"What am I going to do with you, Georgia Black?" Her mother put the supper down on the blue blanket and leaned over to give her a hug. "Are you sure you're going to be OK here overnight, sweetheart?" she asked.

"Definitely," said Georgia determinedly. "I have to stay."

Her mum smiled. "I thought you might say that!"

She sat with Georgia while she ate her food,

asking her questions about the summer school, which Georgia answered as best she could, only blushing slightly when Dan's name came up. Then, when the last remnants had been devoured, her mum got to her feet and ruffled her daughter's hair affectionately. "Be sure to get Melanie if you need her," her mum said, letting herself out of the stable. She paused and looked in over the half-door. "And try to get some sleep, darling."

"I will. Thanks, Mum." Georgia smiled appreciatively.

After her mother had left, Georgia snuggled down into the straw and pulled the blanket over her. She couldn't believe how still the night was now after the drama of earlier. Lily was standing quietly at the back of the stable, resting a leg. She didn't come any closer, but she didn't look scared either.

Georgia was exhausted after the trauma of the last twenty-four hours and although she tried to fight to stay awake to watch the pony, her eyelids grew heavier and heavier. Eventually when, with a small sigh, Lily finally closed her eyes, Georgia allowed herself to drift off to sleep. And later, comforted by the presence of the girl who had shown her such kindness, the palomino pony lay down for the first time in months and slept.

CHAPTER THIRTEEN

When dawn broke, girl and pony were still fast asleep. That was how Melanie found them as the first few rays of sunshine bounced off Lily's coat, turning it a deep pink. Georgia's golden hair, which was spread out in a tangled wave, was full of straw.

"Georgia ... Georgia ... it's time to wake up," Melanie whispered.

Lily started at the sound of her voice and hastily got to her feet. Georgia rubbed her eyes and gazed sleepily around her.

"The vet's popping over before his surgery opens," Melanie said. "If I make you a bacon sandwich, can you feed the ponies?"

"Sure." Georgia nodded, the thought of a bacon sandwich making her mouth water. She was starving, despite the soup and cake Mum had brought her last night.

Leaving Lily's stable, Georgia set to work. She fed Wilson a competition mix and Callie a small handful of pony nuts, before making up a small bran mash for Lily. Then she turned Wilson and Callie out into the paddock, smiling as they rolled together in the dusty earth.

Lily tucked eagerly into her bran mash, keeping an eye on Georgia as she ate. Georgia watched her for a few minutes before setting about mucking out the stables. She skipped out the beds, fluffed up the straw and washed out the feed bowls. She was just finishing off when Melanie emerged from the house, carrying a bacon sandwich and a steaming mug of tea. Georgia took them from her gratefully, just as the vet pulled into the yard.

"How's she doing?" he said, getting out of his car.

"OK, I think," said Melanie. "Georgia stayed with her all night."

"Now, that's dedication!" laughed the vet. "Well, let's take a look at her then." He drew back the bolt on the door and stepped inside. "She was in a very fragile state last night," he said as he checked her pulse. "Has she eaten her bran mash?"

"Yup." Georgia grinned. "She's had it all!"

The vet nodded as he checked Lily's respiration

PaLOMiNO

PONY

and temperature before finally listening to her abdomen with a stethoscope.

"Well, she's much improved," he declared. "You could turn her out if you want."

"Why don't you put her in the small paddock next to Wilson and Callie then, Georgia?" said Melanie.

Carefully, Georgia led Lily out, taking care not to startle her, and unclipped her once they were in the field. Georgia stood back to watch as, hesitantly, Lily stepped forward. In the next moment she had launched herself into a floating extended trot.

"I think you can safely say she's made herself at home." The vet grinned, before heading for his car.

When he had driven away, Melanie turned to Georgia. "Well, I've got good news and bad," she said, looking at her intently.

"OK," Georgia said slowly. She took a deep breath. "Let's start with the good news then."

"All right." Melanie hesitated. "Well, I've phoned the Builth pony sales." She paused. "And I've managed to trace her owner – Mr Williams. He's furious with his granddaughter. Her version of the story was that Lily had turned on her and nearly broken her leg and then run away. But knowing Lily, he'd had his doubts. So he wasn't at all surprised when I told him what had really happened."

"As if Lily would turn on anyone!" Georgia snorted with disgust.

"I know … a likely story, eh?" said Melanie. "Anyway, the good news is that Mr Williams remembered you. And he wants us to have Lily! We've agreed a price and I'm going to send him a cheque."

Georgia gasped. "Wow – that's brilliant!" Then

she looked a bit sheepish. "I hope you haven't had to pay too much."

"She wasn't cheap but she hasn't broken the bank!" Melanie smiled, wrapping an arm around Georgia's shoulder. "But I think she's worth it!"

"Thanks so much, Melanie!" Georgia felt completely overwhelmed. Then she remembered that there was more. "So what's the bad news?" she asked tentatively.

"The bad news," Melanie hesitated, "is the girl – Jemma, Mr Williams's granddaughter. He seems to think that she might cause some trouble when she hears that Lily has gone to you. He said we should watch out for her on the show circuit. Apparently she can be quite difficult."

"But there's nothing she can do, is there?" said Georgia, feeling worried all of a sudden.

"Not a thing," said Melanie. "Not once the cheque has cleared. He was just warning us."

Seeing Georgia's anxious expression, she smiled. "Don't worry, Lily isn't going anywhere. Now, come on, let's go and get to know the newest member of our family!"

✩ ✩ ✩

Later on that day, Emma pushed her bike into the yard, dressed in electric-blue leggings and a baggy purple T-shirt. "So, what do you think?" she said to her best friend, doing a twirl.

"Of what?" asked Georgia, looking up from the piece of tack she had been cleaning. She'd texted Emma earlier and asked her to come over to Redgrove as soon as she could.

"Of me," said Emma. "I've got some new clothes."

"Oh, Em." Georgia laughed, hanging up the clean bridle. "You always look great!" She gave her friend a broad smile. "Come with me. I want you to meet the new arrival."

"New arrival?" said Emma. "The Haydens have a new pony?"

"Yep!" said Georgia. "And she's the best. Oh, Em, I've got so much to tell you!"

In the drama of Lily's arrival, Georgia hadn't had a chance to tell her best friend everything that had happened. That's why she'd texted her at the first opportunity to ask her to come up to the yard.

"It must have been quite a summer course for you to come back this happy," said Emma.

"There was never a dull moment," said Georgia, tucking her arm through her friend's. "Actually, there were loads, but something amazing happened as well."

"Tell me everything," said Emma.

So Georgia did.

Emma's eyes were as wide as saucers when her friend finally stopped for breath. "I can't believe you didn't tell me all of this sooner!" she exclaimed.

"I know, I'm sorry," Georgia said. "But everything happened so quickly. And Dan was really kind and helpful, and he saved Lily's life. He's a complete hero."

"He also happens to be the best-looking guy at our school," Emma pointed out, raising an eyebrow quizzically.

"Is he?" said Georgia nonchalantly. "Well, he's very nice. But I don't think of him like that." She looked thoughtful. Was that entirely true? She thought of Dan as many things – kind and brave and heroic, but boys were really not high on her list of priorities right now, not when she could spend her time looking after ponies. "Come on," she said, leading her friend to the fields at the back. "You need to meet Lily."

the PALOMINO ☆PONY

As they stood at the gate to the small paddock, Emma let out a low whistle of approval. "Wow!" she said, reaching out her hand to where the palomino was grazing close by. Lily immediately moved off and trotted over to the fence at the back of the field, so Georgia reminded Emma why Lily was so skittish.

"That evil girl," her friend murmured with tears in her eyes. "But Lily's safe now, isn't she? Jemma will never get her back!"

"I hope not," Georgia said grimly as they turned to go. She stopped to look over her shoulder at the beautiful pony, resting in the shade of the ancient horse chestnut. It was hard to believe that so much had happened to her.

"I won't ever let you be scared or in danger again, Lily," said Georgia. "I promise you that. Your future's safe with me."

Georgia and Emma walked quietly back to the yard and when Dan showed up half an hour later, as promised, Emma had an inexplicable fit of giggles.

Georgia blushed, noticing for the first time that Emma was right – Dan really was pretty nice-looking! Suddenly overcome with shyness, she took him to visit Lily. He whistled softly as they looked into her paddock. She raised her head and nickered in response.

"See! She remembers you!" Georgia cried in delight, her nerves forgotten. "She knows you're the one who saved her!"

"And you." Dan smiled. "She's lovely, isn't she?" he said. "I can't wait to watch you ride her!"

Emma made a little spluttering sound, and Georgia blushed even more. "Well, that would be great," she said. "But we're going to have to take it really slow after everything she's been through."

Dan nodded. "Well, if you need me, you know where I am," he said kindly, before asking Emma if she wanted him to thump her on the back. "Nasty cough you've got there," he told her, his eyes twinkling. This time it was Emma's turn to blush.

CHAPTER FOURTEEN

The days of summer passed easily. Slowly, Lily
started to get better and settle into life at Redgrove,
and Georgia started to worry about her less and
less. She was managing to catch her quite easily
too now – even if it was with the help of a big
bucket of feed. Georgia loved bringing Lily in for
a groom, stroking her champagne-coloured coat
and talking to her softly.

the PALOMINO ✿PONY

One Saturday morning, as she combed out the little mare's cream mane and tail, Georgia looked thoughtful. "I wonder when someone might try you out, Lily," she breathed. "I wonder who it will be. I'd love it if it was me, but perhaps Sophie would be better. She's much more experienced than I am, you see."

Lily snorted in response and swished her tail. Georgia laughed.

"You'd rather it was me, would you?" she smiled before heading off. "Well, I've got to go and get Wilson ready now but I'll be back. Promise."

Georgia looked back over her shoulder at the palomino, watching her lazily resting one hind leg. She smiled. She was riding Wilson nearly every day now as Sophie seemed to spend most of her time out with her friends, either shopping or sunbathing, but Georgia wasn't complaining.

Still, that day she had a lot to do. Wilson had

119

a big show tomorrow and needed a bath. Then, after she had groomed him, Georgia would need to clean his tack and help Melanie load the lorry ready for their early start. The show was one of the biggest in the calendar and Georgia knew that Wilson had lots of competition from all over the country in his classes.

"Easy, boy, easy does it," Georgia crooned as she lathered up the soap on the bay gelding. Wilson loved his baths and stood quietly under the hose, revelling in the feel of the cool water as Georgia washed his ebony mane with shampoo. He dried in the hot sun in no time and Georgia sprayed conditioner into his tail before combing it out. Finally she ran some special coat shine over him with a soft cloth.

"You look like a star!" she said, giving Wilson a kiss on the nose.

After that was done Georgia polished

Wilson's show tack and prepared all his kit, his grooming brushes, water containers and bandages, remembering to pack some treats as well.

Lily hung her head over her stable door and watched all of the show preparation with interest. "Don't worry, girl," Georgia called as she ran past, her arms full of travelling boots. "It'll be you in the ring one day!"

☆ ☆ ☆

The next morning was the usual frantic rush to get ready in time, but thanks to all of Georgia's preparations the day before they were soon pulling out of the yard and heading off to the show.

Sophie was asleep in the passenger seat. Georgia sat beside her, eating one of the sandwiches her mum had prepared the night before.

"Oh, before I forget, I've got something for you, Georgia." Melanie leaned across and pulled out a little badge from the glove compartment.

"Groom!" Georgia read the word aloud and pinned the badge proudly to her chest. "Thanks, Melanie!"

"You deserve it," said Melanie.

It seemed like no distance at all to the show, and soon the green horse lorry was pulling into the grounds.

Georgia took a deep breath as she looked around her. She loved everything about a show – from the rows of trailers parked up under the trees, to the gleaming horses getting ready for their big moment. She especially loved the hamburgers and ice creams that made up a show-day diet!

She'd been sad to leave Lily that morning, but Simon had promised to check on her at least six times that day, so Georgia knew she would be all right.

Melanie drove the horse lorry into their allotted space and Georgia jumped down ...

straight into a dark-haired girl who was sitting by the adjacent horsebox. Tory! OK, so there had to be one downside to the day. Georgia hadn't seen Tory since the training day at Janey Meadon's, and couldn't say that she was sad about it.

"Hello there." Georgia swallowed hard and tried to be friendly as Tory flicked through a fashion magazine without looking up. "Hello, Georgia." Tory finally acknowledged her with a dismissive flick of her wrist.

"Oh, hi, Tory," Sophie called out, jumping down behind Georgia.

Tory got up and the two older girls disappeared off together to register for their classes and collect their numbers. *Thank goodness for that*, Georgia thought to herself. *Peace and quiet.*

Sophie was riding in the show hunter pony class. It was one of the later, mid-morning events, so at least it would allow Georgia time to give Wilson another good groom.

Georgia tied him up to the side of the lorry in the shade with his hay net. The sun was already beating down on to the showground and she didn't want him to overheat.

Once Georgia had brushed the bay over, Melanie fussed around Wilson's tail, spraying in some more silky shine and combing it out again. "Can you double-check the ring we're in?" she called to Georgia, who was giving the tack a final polish.

"Sure," Georgia replied, grabbing a carton of juice. She was glad she had dressed for the weather, wearing a pair of pale-pink bermuda shorts with a vest top and her old trainers.

She set off to find a steward. Glancing with pleasure at the beautiful show horses being slowly cantered in the warm-up ring, Georgia made her way over to a bowler-hatted man. But then her blood froze at the sound of a familiar, unwelcome voice. She followed the source of the voice and to her horror saw Jemma sitting astride a chestnut Welsh stallion.

The girl was yelling at a younger rider with red hair and freckles who was nervously arranging a jump in the warm-up ring.

"You stupid idiot," Jemma screeched, her cruel, mocking voice carrying loud and clear across the ring. "I told you to bring his other girth!" She dug her heels hard in the chestnut's sides. He gave a snort of displeasure and broke into a canter.

Jemma was sitting upright in the saddle, her hands tightly clenched on the double reins. Georgia noticed at once how Jemma's riding style differed from Sophie's. Her whole body language was hard and unsympathetic, and the horse she was mounted on looked desperately unhappy, his ears tightly pinned back against his head. White foam splattered against his chest, and his eyes were bulging with effort.

Georgia watched Jemma cantering around the arena until she suddenly realised that pretty soon the chestnut was going to come past where she was standing. She tried to turn away but it was too late. As she was about to pass by, Jemma did a double-take.

"I know you, don't I?" she hissed, pulling the chestnut hard in his mouth and bringing him to a standstill. "Where from?"

"I ... I..." Georgia stuttered.

And then, clearly, it dawned on Jemma. "It's you! You're the girl who took Lily! You TOOK my pony!"

Chapter Fifteen

Georgia didn't know what to say. She stared at Jemma for a very long time before finally she managed to stammer, "Lily was injured – she nearly died. We had to get a vet to look at her, but we saved her and we've bought her now."

"Bought her?" Jemma laughed, and the sound was cruel and mocking. "Oh, please," she taunted. "You mean the paltry amount you gave my grandfather? That wasn't payment – that was practically a gift. As far as I'm concerned, she's still mine and I want her back. And what I want I usually get…"

"You can't take Lily from me. Not ever," Georgia said firmly.

But Jemma seemed not to hear her. She pointed at the badge on Georgia's chest, looking her up and down. "What's this then?" she sneered. *"Groom?"*

Georgia opened her mouth to speak, but just then a steward called for the competitors for the Welsh pony class.

Wheeling the chestnut around and digging her heels harshly into his ribs, Jemma cantered away in a cloud of dust, but not before she delivered her parting shot. "I'll get that pony back, just you wait and see!"

Georgia's heart felt like it was drumming in her

ears. She raced back along the dry ground to the lorry where she ran head first into Melanie, who was rolling up Wilson's travelling bandages.

"What is it? Whatever's the matter, Georgia?" Melanie asked, sounding worried. "Have we missed the class?"

"No, no it's not that." Georgia shook her head.

Pale and shaking, Georgia told her everything that had just happened. When she'd finished, Melanie's mouth was set in a thin line. "Well, take no notice. There's nothing that girl can do," she said firmly. "Lily belongs to me now; she hasn't got a leg to stand on. Honestly, Georgia, I've had her papers from the Welsh Pony Society and everything. Lily is ours. Try and forget about her. She can't take Lily back, she just can't."

Sophie emerged from the horse lorry at that moment, looking beautiful in her canary-yellow breeches and tailored jacket, with her long hair tucked into a hair net.

"What's this?" she asked.

"It's nothing." Georgia turned away, hiding her tears. She busied herself with Wilson, tacking him up and giving his coat a final polish. Regardless of Melanie's reassuring words, she couldn't forget the threat in Jemma's voice.

Despite her worries, out of the corner of her eye Georgia noticed Tory slipping out of her horsebox and crossing the lorry park where she started talking to an older-looking boy. Georgia frowned. He seemed vaguely familiar. Curious, she turned to Sophie, who was arranging her tie in the lorry mirror.

"Who's that boy?" she asked.

Sophie followed her gaze and shrugged, her eyes slightly downcast as she swung up on to Wilson. "Don't ask me. Tory knows everyone at these shows. She's always going off to see someone or other."

Georgia couldn't help but notice the way Tory threw a filthy look in their direction even though she was still deep in conversation. Was she talking about Georgia? Or perhaps she and Sophie had had a falling-out?

Still, there wasn't time to think about that now. Sophie had started to warm Wilson up under Melanie's meticulous eye and Georgia wanted to watch. Shortly afterwards, the show hunter pony class was called and Sophie headed off on Wilson. Georgia made her way to the ringside with Melanie to watch.

To Georgia's horror, as she took her seat she realised that Jemma was in the class as well, this time mounted on a beautiful dark-grey gelding.

Georgia tried not to look at her, choosing to focus on the other horses instead. Wilson was behaving beautifully, his trot fluid, his tightly plaited mane showing off the perfect curve of his neck and gleaming conker coat.

But as he trotted round, Jemma kept trying to overtake him. It looked as though she was determined to ruin his show as she brushed past him with just millimetres to spare.

Wilson spooked sideways, his ears back, his tail swishing.

Georgia felt uneasy. Jemma was clever, covering her actions with a big smile whenever the judge was looking her way, so he didn't see what was going on. Eventually Jemma was pulled in first and Sophie second.

"I'm going to make an official complaint," Melanie fumed as Sophie and Wilson came out of the ring.

"What's going on? Who was that girl?" Sophie cried, clearly shaken.

Georgia felt terrible. It was all her fault. She opened her mouth to say something, then closed it again, lost for words.

✧ ✧ ✧

For the rest of the day, Georgia tried to forget about Jemma and her threats to take Lily back. After all, Melanie had made it clear that she was the rightful owner now. Even so, Georgia felt a shiver run down her spine whenever she thought about it. She washed Wilson down and tied him up with a hay net before going off to have a quick wander around the showground, leaving Melanie with the horses. Melanie had met a friend and the two of them were chatting in picnic chairs outside the horse lorry.

She would have to keep her eyes peeled for Jemma. She didn't want to run into her again.

"We'll leave in about half an hour, Georgia," Melanie called after her. "Go and enjoy yourself."

Georgia loved having the chance to look around. Every show was different, and today's show was no exception. She admired the sheep with their impressive horns and the Dexter cows in the livestock pens, before gazing wistfully at the long-haired rabbits in the pet tent. Georgia would have liked to have had a rabbit of her own but her mum always said it was too risky with a dog around. She bought an ice cream and a can of cola from a stall and was just wandering back through the line of horseboxes when a voice from the other side of a dark-maroon lorry made her stop in her tracks.

"I'd know that girl anywhere..."

It was Jemma.

Quickly tucking herself into the shadows of the horsebox, Georgia held her breath. Jemma was sitting in the doorway to the livestock entrance, flanked by two older boys. She couldn't see their faces, but she was sure they were the boys

Georgia had seen her with on the field trip. Her blood ran cold at the sound of their voices and she shuddered at the thought of the three of them closing in on Lily on the mountainside, ready to beat her if she disobeyed.

"Nobody makes me look a fool. I want that pony back." Jemma's voice was snarling and menacing.

Georgia shrank further into the shadows of the horsebox, straining to hear the rest of the conversation.

"That little upstart thinks she can get one over on me," Jemma continued, her voice growing angrier. "But I'm not going to let her get away with it! That stupid pony was given to me, and I'll do what I like with her!"

"But your granddad sold her, didn't he?" said one of the boys.

"Oh, for goodness' sake!" Jemma snapped, sounding as if she was going to explode.

"Granddad's done with the ponies! He's totally lost the plot! Mum and I are taking over the business now!"

One of the boys spoke again, sounding worried. "But they'll be able to find out if you've taken the pony. You'll get done for stealing."

Jemma's voice was quieter now, like a white rage. "Then I'll just say Granddad's soft in the head so it doesn't count … that he didn't sell the pony at all. I'm sure there's no contract or anything. Now, are you with me or not? Because you're both sounding as pathetic as anything right now!"

The boys mumbled a reply that Georgia could just about make out as a yes before she sprinted back across to the Haydens' horsebox, her heart pounding and her mouth dry with fear.

When Georgia told Melanie all about the conversation she had just overheard, Melanie looked a bit exasperated. "Look, Georgia, she's

136

definitely a nasty piece of work," she said, "but she won't come to the stables to steal Lily. She'll have more sense than that."

Georgia hung her head. She knew Melanie thought she was silly to worry but she hadn't heard the steely determination in the girl's voice.

Melanie softened. "Listen, don't worry. We'll watch out for her at shows from now on, just in case she tries to make trouble. OK?"

Georgia nodded.

"I can't have her upsetting my number-one groom now, can I?" Melanie ruffled Georgia's hair. "Now, come on. Let's get this horse lorry on the road."

Georgia gave Melanie a small smile, but she couldn't ignore the knot of anxiety still twisting in her stomach. What if Jemma really did carry out her threat? What if she came and tried to take Lily away? Georgia knew she couldn't bear that.

Suddenly Georgia's head went up. She just wasn't going to ignore what she'd heard. If Melanie didn't believe her, then it was up to Georgia to keep Lily safe. She'd made a promise to the little palomino and she was going to keep it, whatever happened.

CHAPTER SIXTEEN

"There you are, my angel," Georgia called as she got out of the horse lorry and ran across the yard at Redgrove. It had seemed a much longer journey back from the show and it was such a relief to see the little pony again, safe and sound, standing at the gate with Callie.

Lily gave a shrill whinny as Melanie unboxed Wilson. She was clearly delighted to see the handsome bay pony. Georgia placed both arms around the mare's neck, breathing in her scent and the warmth of the early evening sunshine on her golden coat.

"Boy, am I glad to see you!" she murmured. The little pony stood stock still, responding to Georgia's touch. It was amazing to think that just a few weeks ago no one could go near her.

Melanie came over and patted Lily softly on her muzzle. "You know, I've been thinking. Maybe it's time you had a go at riding her."

"Me? Really?" Georgia cried, delighted. "You think she's ready? You think she might let me?"

"I don't see why not," said Melanie. "She trusts you. You can see that. And that's a good starting point."

Georgia knew that Melanie was probably bringing this up now to make her feel better about everything that had happened at the show, but she

140

wasn't about to complain.

"What do you say? Shall we give it a go tomorrow?" Melanie said. "After that, Sophie and I are away for a few days, visiting universities. So you should definitely try her out before then. What do you think?"

"I think it sounds great!" Georgia grinned.

✿ ✿ ✿

The next morning, Georgia bounded out of bed. Melanie's promise from the day before was still ringing in her ears. Today was the day she was going to try out Lily! What would she be like? Would she be easy to ride? Would her stride be as fluid from above as it looked from below? Dressing quickly in jodhs and her favourite purple T-shirt, Georgia pulled a comb through her tangle of hair and, grabbing a piece of toast, she quickly headed for the door.

"Bye, Mum!"

"Bye, Georgia!" her mum called back as the door swung shut behind her.

Georgia cycled quickly down the quiet lanes and as she made her way up the drive to Redgrove she was pleased to see all three ponies in the paddock grazing quietly together. They made a beautiful trio – the dark, elegant Wilson; Lily, the pretty palomino; and the small Exmoor, Callie, her dun coat gleaming in the early morning light. Georgia sighed. She was so lucky to be allowed to care for these ponies as if they were her own.

To her surprise, Sophie was out in the yard cleaning Wilson's tack, which was hanging over the gate. She looked up when she saw Georgia.

"Hey," she called in a friendly voice. "You're going to ride Lily today, aren't you?"

"I think so!" Georgia replied, pleased at Sophie's sudden interest.

"I think she's lovely," Sophie continued.

The two girls smiled at one other before Georgia went into the tack room to fetch Lily's head collar.

As Georgia let herself into the field, the little pony whickered and slowly approached, flanked by Callie, who was bossily protective of her now. Carefully, Georgia placed a head collar on the palomino and then led her into the yard.

"She's looking lovely," Melanie called, appearing from the house clutching a cup of tea. "So are you ready to give it a go?"

"Yes, I think so!" Georgia replied, feeling terrified and elated at the same time. She really hoped Lily was going to be OK with being ridden.

"Great!" Melanie said. "Well, I've made up a little bridle for her, and the old show saddle should fit her too – at least for now. So let's try her at a walk to start with, and see how she goes."

Very carefully, not wanting to startle her, Georgia tacked Lily up, admiring the way the brown leather looked against her pale coat. She put on her navy riding hat and fastened the chinstrap, and then, very gently, she untied Lily's lead rope and led her over to the mounting block.

Melanie held Lily's head while Georgia carefully eased herself into the saddle. She sat quietly for a moment, hardly daring to breathe, feeling the pony tremble beneath her. "You're safe now, girl," she murmured, reaching down and running her hand through the palomino's cream mane.

Melanie watched intently, ready to act if Lily panicked. But she didn't.

Slowly, sitting as still as a statue, her hands making feather-light contact, Georgia nudged the palomino and she obediently walked forwards. They rode through the gate and then up the path alongside the stables, which was cool and shaded by heavily laden elderflower bushes.

"Easy, girl," Georgia soothed. Breathing in the

summer scents and enjoying the easy rhythm of the Welsh pony, she started to relax.

Melanie walked next to them, never taking her eyes off the pair as they walked past the house and into the open meadow. Lily was walking out now, her stride fluid, as if she was floating.

"You little star!" Melanie praised the pony, whose ears were now pricked forward. "Why don't you try a lap?" she encouraged Georgia.

Feeling as if she might burst with happiness, Georgia nudged Lily forward. Then, once they had circled the meadow a couple more times, she steered Lily back to the yard.

There she dismounted and flung her arms round the little mare, covering her with kisses. "I love you so much!" she said as she buried her face into the pony's golden neck, almost crying with joy. Jemma's alarming words forgotten now, Georgia felt as though she and Lily could do anything.

Nothing could spoil their happiness!

From now on, she would ride Lily every day until she had restored the palomino's natural confidence. After that, there would be the prospect of shows and Pony Club camps, long summer rides and winter hacks. It was going to be amazing!

✩ ✩ ✩

Later that afternoon, as Georgia helped Melanie in the garden, she spotted Sophie and Tory sunbathing by the pool. Tory was tapping away at her mobile and ignoring Sophie's attempts at conversation.

It was odd, really. Tory seemed to be popping in a lot at the moment but never staying for very long. And she was always glammed up nowadays, as if she was ready for a night out. Today was no exception. She was wearing a short denim miniskirt and a yellow vest, her make-up applied thickly, which made her look

much older than seventeen.

Sophie sighed and turned over on to her stomach just as Tory suddenly leapt up, grabbed her bag and left, as if she had just received an urgent text. Barely bothering to say goodbye, she stalked out of the garden, her phone glued to her ear.

Melanie watched, a frown on her face. "She's a strange girl, that Tory," she said confidentially to Georgia. "When Sophie starts university I'm hoping their friendship might fizzle out."

Georgia watched Tory as she left the yard. She'd never liked her but what could she say? It was interesting to know that Melanie felt the same though. Georgia couldn't help thinking that there was something a bit suspicious about Tory's behaviour lately and there was always the worry that the older girl was going to say something mean to her. Still, with Melanie and Sophie away for the next few days, Tory wouldn't be around at

Redgrove. Georgia sighed happily. She wouldn't have to think about a single thing apart from her beloved ponies.

CHAPTER SEVENTEEN

"Bye, Georgia! See you in three days!" Melanie got into the driver's seat of the four-by-four, Sophie by her side. Then, as an afterthought, she rolled down her window. "Are you sure you'll be all right, looking after the horses by yourself? Simon will only be here in the evenings, remember."

"I'll be just fine," Georgia assured her. "Now, off you go!"

"OK." Melanie nodded. "Well, thank you. Just text me if there are any problems, won't you?"

"I will." Georgia smiled. "Although there won't be," she added. "Em and Dan are going to come and visit and help me out."

Georgia waved as the four-by-four disappeared down the drive. She couldn't believe that Melanie trusted her enough to leave her in charge of the ponies. It was brilliant!

Pip, who had run alongside her bike as she cycled over to Redgrove that morning, was at her heel as she turned back to the yard. "Come on, girl. Let's go and check on the ponies," she said happily, rubbing her between the ears.

The three of them were standing in their shelter, eyes closed, heads hanging as they lazily swatted flies away with their tails. There was a faint hum of bees in the distance, and the sickly-sweet perfume from the nearby oilseed rape fields, now a vibrant

yellow, hung heavily in the air.

Georgia gave each pony a pat and then counted the chickens to ensure they were all present and correct, scratching around in the dusty earth beside the stable yard. Happy that all the animals were content and peaceful, Georgia made her way into the cool of the house. She had a couple of hours to spare until it was time to give the ponies their supper, and with Emma and Dan both busy for the afternoon she thought she'd read for a while.

Settling herself on the kitchen sofa, she took out her book, shading her eyes against the afternoon sun. Pip stayed in the cool by the back door, idly thumping her tail at Georgia. It was warm in the kitchen and gradually Georgia felt herself growing sleepy.

She could only have been asleep an hour at most, when all of a sudden she was woken by ferocious barking. Pip was on her feet, hackles rising and teeth bared, flanked by the terriers, who were growling at her side. Feeling a chill run through her, Georgia raced out of the back door and, seeing nothing unusual, quickly made her way round the side of the house to the front door.

A boy was standing there, seemingly just about to ring the doorbell. She didn't know him from the village and he didn't look like he was delivering anything. He was wiry and medium height, with dark hair. For some reason he kept glancing around, as if on the lookout for something. Georgia instantly felt uneasy, but politely asked him what he wanted.

"I'm looking for Mrs Hayden," the boy answered. Georgia noticed that he smirked as he said these words. He was definitely behaving strangely.

She thought fast. "Mrs Hayden's out at the moment. But she'll be back later," she added confidently. "Can I give her a message?"

The boy stared at Georgia for a long moment, before looking past her at the paddock beyond the house where Wilson, Lily and Callie were watching the visitor with interest. "Nice horses, those," he said. "Especially the palomino – bet she's worth a bob or two."

Georgia opened her mouth to reply but no words came out.

The boy laughed quietly to himself as he turned back down the drive and walked off.

What was all that about? Georgia thought. *Don't be silly*, she told herself firmly. *It was probably nothing.* Even so, she felt quite shaken as she walked quickly towards the ponies. She checked her watch. It was half past five. She'd call Dan.

"Georgia?" Dan answered his phone straight away. "I was just on my way up."

Quickly Georgia told Dan all about the boy and their weird conversation.

153

"Look, don't panic," he said reassuringly. "I'm sure it's nothing. But I'll be with you in five minutes."

✩ ✩ ✩

When Dan appeared through the yard gates that afternoon, Georgia didn't think she had ever felt so pleased to see anyone. She ran over to him and greeted him exuberantly, much to his amusement.

"There's really nothing to worry about," he said confidently. "We get unexpected visitors all the time on the farm. They usually turn out to be sales reps."

"But this wasn't a sales rep!" Georgia exclaimed. "I'm sure of it. He was far too young, for a start."

"All right, all right," said Dan. "Listen, I've been thinking about what Jemma said. If you're still worried, well…" He indicated a large canvas bag that he'd left by the gates.

"What's that?" said Georgia, puzzled.

"Tents," Dan replied. "I borrowed them from my brother. I thought we could keep watch over the ponies tonight. If your mum agrees, of course. And we'd need to check it out with Simon, but I can't see why he'd mind, can you?"

"That is a brilliant plan!" Georgia smiled warmly at Dan. He was so thoughtful!

"And not only that, but I've brought sleeping bags and food too." He tapped the rucksack that he had slung over his shoulder.

"You've thought of everything!" said Georgia enthusiastically. "I'll see if Em wants to join us," she added, not wanting to leave her best friend out. "I'll go and call her now, after I've spoken to Mum and Simon."

"Good idea," said Dan. "So where shall we put them?" he called after Georgia as she headed for the house.

"Maybe over there," she replied, pointing to the

lawn that was nearest the ponies.

"OK, I'll get started." Dan grinned, striding over to pick up the tent bag.

By the time Georgia got back from speaking to her mum and Simon, Dan had finished putting the two tents up. She'd also rung Emma, who'd jumped at the chance to join them camping and whose mum had agreed straight away, so Dan suggested the two girls share the larger tent.

"This is going to be fun!" he said, standing back to admire his handiwork. "It's not often I get a night away from the farm. I might even get a lie-in!"

Georgia smiled, but she still couldn't shake the uneasy feeling that she'd had ever since that strange boy had turned up. It would be fun to camp with her friends but she also felt a strong sense of foreboding...

Still, she knew she'd feel a lot better that night if

she were actually here with the ponies rather than fretting about them in her bed at home.

☆ ☆ ☆

Georgia began to feel better as the quiet afternoon wore on. Once the ponies had been fed and the picnic devoured, the three friends sat down on the grass with the dogs. Dan had a terrier on his lap and was stroking its tan ears, gently pulling them through his fingers.

Feeling content, Georgia glanced at the ponies, who had just ambled over to them and were now vying for attention over the fence.

Lily hung back shyly, but came forward when Georgia got to her feet and beckoned her gently.

"You know, Georgia, even I can see how much that pony likes you," Emma said, watching her friend gently stroke the pony's curved ears.

"I know," Georgia replied, feeling a little emotional. "I'm so lucky. She's the best thing that's happened to me for a long time!" She cleared her throat and smiled at her friends brightly. "Now, do either of you fancy a game of tennis?"

✿ ✿ ✿

The evening passed quickly. Emma and Dan played tennis on the Haydens' court while Georgia stayed near the ponies, lying on her stomach and keeping one eye on the game and the other on Lily, who hadn't left the fence.

Later, as the sun set and the evening grew chillier, they all wrapped themselves in blankets, lying on their backs to admire the cloudless night sky and the thousands of stars twinkling overhead.

"This is so magical, isn't it?" said Em, gazing up.

"It really is," said Georgia.

The ponies were all asleep by now, Callie lying down, and Wilson and Lily resting their back legs, their heads hanging low and their bottom lips drooping.

Watching the ponies sleeping suddenly made Georgia feel tired and she announced she was going to bed. She crawled into the tent and wriggled into her sleeping bag, followed by Emma and Pip, who curled up on his dog blanket.

"Night, all!" Dan called cheerfully from his tent. "Sleep well!"

⭐ ✩ ⭐

But Georgia didn't sleep well at all. She woke several times, thinking she could hear something. But when she strained her ears, there was nothing. Each time she lay still for a few minutes, before dropping off to sleep again. Pip was dozing beside her, twitching as she dreamed. Emma was also fast asleep, her breathing deep and even.

When Georgia next woke, she glanced at her watch. Ten past three. Suddenly she knew what had woken her – there was a rustling sound outside. Georgia sat up. She could hear the ponies stamping their feet and recognised Wilson's snort.

Creeping out of her tent, she could just about make out the pale form of Lily, who was standing in between Wilson and Callie. All three ponies had their heads high, staring at something in the distance. Just then a fox barked, an eerie sound that carried clearly across the still night sky. The ponies started, shying sideways and snorting. At this, Dan appeared from his tent as well.

"Couldn't you sleep either?" he said in a low voice.

"I thought I heard something," Georgia whispered back.

They both stood still, listening hard. The ponies were quieter now, and Wilson and Callie looked calm. Yet Lily's neck was still arched, and she appeared to be gazing at something unseen in the inky black distance. The little palomino looked as mystical as a unicorn, her white mane sparkling in the moonlight.

Dan crawled closer to Georgia to reassure her. It felt weird sitting so close to a boy but he was warm and solid, and his presence was comforting.

"It was probably just a fox," said Dan. He turned to face Georgia in the gloom. "Listen, nothing is going to happen to those ponies," he said. "Especially not to Lily. I'm too attached to that pony of yours now, after saving her life!"

Georgia mumbled her agreement. "I still don't think I can go back to sleep," she said eventually.

"Nor me," said Dan. "I'll sit up with you, if you like."

And so the two of them fetched their sleeping bags and sat quietly for the rest of the night, watching the ponies until the first rays of sunshine broke over the fields, bathing them in a warm pink glow.

CHAPTER EIGHTEEN

Georgia felt stiff and tired by the time morning dawned properly. After the three friends had breakfasted on the remains of their picnic and drunk the hot mugs of tea that Simon brought out to them, she decided to take a shower to wake herself up. It would have to be a quick one as she wanted to exercise the ponies before it got too hot.

"I've got to go home to help Dad with the cows,"

Dan said apologetically. "But I'll come back later."

"That would be great," said Georgia. "See you then, and thanks for everything."

"I can stay and help out," Emma offered. "I could ride Wilson while you take out Lily, so you're not on your own."

"Fantastic," said Georgia gratefully.

So after Georgia had showered, the two of them rode out, keeping to the woods rather than the open fields. They still only managed an hour before the heat got too much for them. It was going to be a blisteringly hot day.

To Georgia's surprise, Tory was waiting in the yard when they rode back in. She was lounging against the yard gate, wearing skin-tight breeches and a fitted black T-shirt. Her long dark hair was drawn back in a sleek ponytail and she had dark glasses covering her eyes. Pushing herself upright she strode over to

Georgia, who felt Lily tense beneath her.

"Where's Sophie?" she demanded, not even bothering to say hello.

"Sophie?" Georgia frowned, surprised that Tory didn't know where her friend was. "She's not here. She's gone to look at universities with Melanie."

A slight smile curled on Tory's lip but it wasn't a particularly welcoming smile. "Has she now?" she said, moving a bit closer to Lily, who took a sudden step backwards.

"Hey! Careful!" Georgia said. "You're unsettling her." She jumped down and took hold of Lily's reins, brushing past Tory as she led her off.

"How's that palomino doing then? Still a bit skittish, is she?" Tory's voice called after her.

"Lily's just fine, thanks," Georgia replied firmly, glancing back as she reached the mare's stable.

"Good…" Tory's face broke into an unnerving

smile. "Well, be sure to tell Sophie I dropped by, won't you?"

Wondering why Tory couldn't tell Sophie herself, Georgia watched the older girl as she turned on her heel and strode purposefully out of the yard. Tory opened the door of a silver sports car that had been waiting in the lane outside and slid into the passenger seat. Georgia couldn't tell who was driving but it definitely wasn't Tory's mum. The driver was male, as far as she could make out, and had a baseball cap pulled low over his face.

"What was that all about?" Emma exclaimed.

"I don't know," Georgia replied, feeling a familiar cold chill run down her spine, "but I intend to find out…"

☆ ☆ ☆

There was a lot to do in the yard, and the girls tried to forget about Tory's visit as they got stuck into their jobs. Even when everything was done,

Georgia found herself sweeping the yard all over again in an attempt to distract her from thinking about Tory's words.

Eventually, feeling hot and sticky, the girls decided it was time to cool off in the Haydens' swimming pool. Georgia quickly changed into her swimming costume and plunged into the clear water. She swam a few lengths and then spread herself out on a towel next to Emma and lay on her stomach, gazing out at the paddock. The swim had done her good. And the ponies looked so peaceful, so serene. Perhaps she was just worrying unnecessarily after all.

At six o'clock on the dot, Dan strode through the yard gates.

"Hey, girls," he called. "All OK?"

"Not so bad," Georgia called back, scrunching up her eyes in the evening sun. Dan's hair was still wet from his shower and he was wearing shorts and a frayed shirt. Georgia watched him pause at the fence to stroke the ponies, who jostled for his attention.

A little later, once the ponies and dogs had been fed for the evening, and the chickens put away, the three friends flopped on to the grass.

"Who's for a drink?" asked Dan, producing some glasses and ice he'd fetched from the house and opening a bottle of cola.

"Me!" said Emma. "I'm parched!"

"Me too," said Georgia, gratefully accepting a drink. "Oh, Dan, you know what? A strange thing happened today…" She quickly filled him in on Tory's visit.

"It was like she was checking up on us or something," Emma said finally, "and she didn't even seem to know that Sophie had gone away."

Dan shrugged. "That's weird, if they're supposed to be such good friends. Maybe they've had a bust-up."

"Maybe," said Georgia, shrugging. "Anyway, shall we all camp out again tonight? Simon doesn't mind, and he's away overnight for work anyway. Mum said I could if you two were up for it. And she said she'd drop off some food if I let her know."

"Yup, I'm in," said Em. "I'll let my parents know."

"That makes three of us!" Dan added. "Dad won't mind."

☆ ☆ ☆

After the scorching-hot day it was another warm, pleasant evening. It had been so dry of late that the grass was starting to turn yellow and there were cracks appearing in the hard ground.

Emma took charge of preparing their supper once Georgia's mum had dropped off supplies. They had baguettes with cold meats and cheese

followed by chocolate brownies and fresh peaches. Em dug out her iPod and speakers from her bag and they spent another happy evening singing and laughing together. Georgia was really enjoying herself but she still had that niggling feeling that something was wrong. To try to put her mind at rest, she sent a text to Sophie to let her know that Tory had been round, hoping that Sophie's response would make everything clear.

But Sophie didn't reply. They must have gone out for the evening. With a sigh, Georgia put her phone back in the tent and tried to get into the spirit of things with her friends.

☆ ☆ ☆

It wasn't until later that night, when everyone was sleeping, that Georgia woke with a start. What was that noise? It sounded like a car pulling up in the lane. Georgia felt her heart beating. It *was* a car pulling up in the lane! She could just about make out muffled voices, and footsteps. Quickly she grabbed her phone, which was flashing with a text message. It was from Sophie.

Thought Tory on hols in Spain this week???!!!

Now Georgia knew something was wrong.

Hurriedly waking Emma, she pulled on her boots over her pyjamas and crawled out of the tent.

"Dan … Dan…" she whispered, trying to keep the rising panic out of her voice. "Dan, wake up!"

"Urrgh. What time is it?" Dan answered, crawling out of his tent.

"It's gone midnight," said Georgia. "Listen, can you hear that?"

They huddled together, trying to work out where the voices were coming from.

"OK," Dan said authoritatively. "I'm going to go to the front of the house; you two get to the ponies!"

Georgia and Emma did as they were told, sprinting across the garden, climbing over the gate and into the field.

To Georgia's relief, all three ponies were at the far end of the paddock.

"It's all right, Em," she whispered. "They're all right."

"But look!" Emma hissed.

Georgia looked over to the far side of the field into the shadows beneath the trees. She gasped. There were two figures climbing over the fence from the road!

CHAPTER NINETEEN

"Go and get Dan! And bring the ponies' head-collars from the tack room!" Georgia whispered urgently to Emma, who immediately turned and ran off to the yard.

As if sensing sudden danger, all three ponies trotted over to Georgia, Wilson snorting, and Lily and Callie quivering. She tried to calm them by whispering to them but the ponies

were definitely skittish.

Steeling herself, Georgia stood guard in front of the animals and watched the figures approaching. With a jolt of fear she realised they were the same boys that had been with Jemma on the mountainside. Even worse, one of them was carrying a rope in his hands. They were coming for Lily! Georgia felt anger growing inside her. How dare they try to steal the little palomino! She took a deep breath and drew herself up tall, her rage masking her fear.

"You again," one of the boys sneered. "Now, are you going to play nice or are we going to have to deal with you first?"

"You are *not* taking her," Georgia said loudly. "She belongs here and I won't let you have her." She tried to keep the panic out of her voice and glanced towards the house for any sign of Emma. Where was she? And where was Dan?

"Now, come on," the boy said a little more gently. "We don't want to hurt you, but we're here to take back what doesn't belong to you. This is Jemma's pony. She's missed her!"

Georgia could almost have laughed at this statement if it wasn't so threatening.

"She's not Jemma's pony any more!" she argued. "She was sold to us, remember!"

"Well, according to Jem, she wasn't," the other boy broke in now. "Her granddad's been losing it, you see. He doesn't know what he's saying any more. Jemma and her mum run the business now – buying, selling, breeding—"

"And beating up ponies?" Georgia hissed, her body shaking with fear and anger.

"Look," the boy continued, his voice growing more impatient as he coiled the heavy rope in his hands. "I suggest you just get out of our way before we have to make you."

Lily was still behind Georgia, and as the boys stepped forward, she reared. The boys, who were clearly not horsemen, retreated nervously.

"Get out of my way," the older of the two boys growled at Georgia, suddenly lunging at her. She screamed as his rough hands grabbed her arm. Pulling backward she took a handful of a now-terrified Lily's mane, kicking out with both feet.

Before he could react, Georgia had swung herself on to Lily's back. Closing both legs tightly around her sides, she entwined her hands in the white mane. "Go!" she yelled.

The palomino leapt forward into a half-rear before galloping straight between the two boys, forcing them to jump sideways to avoid her flying hooves.

Girl and pony thundered across the length of the paddock, a flash of gold as Georgia gripped on for dear life. Wilson and Callie were following in a cloud of dust, their manes and tails streaming behind them.

As Georgia reached the fence that divided the paddock from the meadows beyond, she whirled Lily round to face the boys. They were running now, their faces red with anger, as they shouted instructions to a third boy who had suddenly appeared and was approaching from the other side of the field. To Georgia's horror, he was twirling a lunge whip in his hands and what looked like a piece of hessian, which he clearly intended to use to blindfold Lily!

Looking frantically around, Georgia spotted a cattle trailer parked in the lane and for the first time ever she wished that the Haydens lived a little closer to a main road. There was no way anyone in the village would be able to hear the commotion.

Where *was* everyone? Georgia hoped that

Emma had found Dan and prayed that they weren't in any danger.

Just then, as Georgia wheeled Lily round to face the yard, she heard a muffled scream. It was Emma! Georgia could just make out that it had come from the tack room and through the gloom she could see a tall, dark-haired girl pressing against the door and fumbling with the padlock.

Tory! What on earth was she doing here?

But there wasn't time to think about that now. One of the boys was trying to herd Wilson and Callie back into the yard so that they could close in on her and Lily. They were trapped.

"Are you going to hand her over? Or are we going to have to pull you off?" the younger boy asked again.

In one last desperate attempt, Georgia turned Lily again and squeezed hard on her sides, aiming her at the post and rail fence. The palomino burst into a canter and quickly covered the ground. Then, for one moment, Lily hesitated, but before Georgia had time to think about how high the fence was, the little pony had tucked her hooves into her chest and soared over, clearing it as gracefully as a bird.

Laughing with delight despite her terror, Georgia and Lily galloped through the meadow, the long grasses brushing Georgia's feet as they raced and raced. They were safe! They just needed to reach the footpath and they'd have a clear run round to the front of the house.

All of a sudden, headlights dazzled Georgia and a four-by-four descended fast upon them. Lily veered sharply to the right and Georgia fell hard to the ground. She was aware of shouting and of Lily's frightened whinny, and then the faint wail of sirens. After that, everything went black, and she sank into darkness…

Chapter Twenty

Georgia felt as if she was swimming in treacle. Everything was thick and heavy and it was hard to move. She could see the sky above her and she knew she was lying on the ground, but she didn't have the energy to get up. Her whole body felt like lead and pain was flooding through her left arm. She was swathed in darkness but there was light ahead, and what was that? Was it Dan's voice?

Suddenly everything was so bright, it hurt her eyes, piercing her senses. Dan was shouting now, his voice was loud and he sounded upset.

"Georgia! Georgia! I'm here."

"What?" Georgia's voice was groggy.

"Don't move her!" said another voice, an older voice that Georgia didn't recognise.

"Georgia, you're awake!" Dan was gripping her hand now. "It's OK, the ambulance is here! It's going to be OK!"

Ambulance? A jolt ran through Georgia but she was too weak to move. "Lily!" she gasped, her lips cracked and dry.

"Lily's fine," Dan said firmly. "Sophie has her. She and Melanie got home early. I'll explain when you're OK!"

Georgia felt herself being loaded on to a stretcher at this point, but even in her dazed state, relief flooded her body.

✿ ✿ ✿

Two hours later, Georgia was sitting up in hospital.
Miraculously, her head was fine, even though
the doctors had suspected concussion. She had
an angry purple bruise across her cheek and her
wrist was broken. The room was full of people –
her mother, gripping on to her good hand, Dan,
Emma, Melanie and Sophie.

"You did it, Georgia!" said Emma. "You scared
them off!"

Georgia's mother laid a hand on her daughter's
arm. "Slowly, Em," she breathed. "Tell her slowly."

Emma nodded and then carefully fitted together
the puzzle of the night's events. First of all,
Melanie and Sophie, made suspicious by Tory's
behaviour and concerned for everyone's welfare
as Simon was away, had headed home early. En
route to Redgrove Farm, they had received a
frantic call from Tory's mum who had overheard

her daughter discussing the night's plans with her new boyfriend.

Sophie, who had long suspected that Tory was dating one of the boys that Jemma hung round with, called the police.

Then, when Emma had gone to find Dan, Tory had managed to lock both of them up in the tack room.

"Those boys fled at the sight of the police cars. And me and Em were very pleased when the police let us out!" said Dan, smiling at Georgia.

"It sounds like a TV drama!" she managed to joke, now that she knew everyone was safe.

"A drama that ended well, thankfully," Georgia's mum said, her eyes full of concern. "Things could have turned out terribly. I had no idea that you were going to be there without Simon otherwise I'd never have agreed to let you camp. I shall pay a lot more attention to things from now on…" She trailed off, tears welling up in her eyes.

"I'm sorry, Mum," Georgia croaked, squeezing her mum's hand. "You've been so busy, I haven't wanted to bother you."

"Well, it's all turned out for the best," Lucy Black smiled weakly. "And if you hadn't been there, Jemma would have been halfway back to Wales now, with Lily."

Jemma! thought Georgia in panic.

"It's OK, Georgia," Dan said quickly, as if reading her mind. "The police caught Jemma heading to the railway station! She thought she could hide there and catch the first train back to Wales."

Georgia felt a wave of relief wash over her. The police had Jemma! There was no way now that she would be able to take Lily!

Melanie, who had waited patiently while everyone said their piece, spoke for the first time.

"I'm going down to the police station tomorrow with the letter I have from Jemma's grandfather and Lily's documents. It'll prove she belongs to me and Jemma won't be able to bother us again. They take this kind of theft very seriously, especially as those boys threatened you."

Georgia shuddered, remembering how they had closed in on her and Lily, and the palomino's brave leap for freedom.

"You know, Lily didn't leave your side after you fell," Melanie added gently. "She must really love you."

Georgia's mother gently stroked her daughter's hair. "Melanie and I have been planning something." She smiled. "We were going to wait, but now is as good a time as any." She turned to Melanie. "Why don't you tell her?"

"Tell me what?" Georgia looked from one woman to the other, totally confused.

"I'd like you to have Lily on loan," said Melanie. "She can stay at the yard but essentially she's yours."

"Really?" Georgia blinked, unbelieving. This was beyond her wildest dreams.

"Yes, really," said Melanie. "You are so dedicated to that pony. You deserve it and it's all been decided. You can earn her keep by helping with the ponies."

"And my paintings are selling OK now," said Georgia's mum. "So we can afford her feed and shoes."

Georgia didn't know what to say. Her own pony – on loan! "Thank you so much! That is the best news I've had in my whole life!" Georgia attempted to sit up to hug Melanie, but she felt too weak.

Melanie patted her hand. "You two have formed such a special bond," she said. "She still needs to regain her full confidence, but I think that you can help her do that and eventually she'll make a top-class show pony. So what do you think?"

Georgia could barely speak; her throat felt lumpy, and tears pricked her eyes. "It's the best," she whispered. Then she turned to her mum. "And thank you so much too. I promise I won't let you down – with my schoolwork, I mean."

Georgia's mum smiled and squeezed her hand, her eyes full of tears too. "I'll hold you to that, young lady. And maybe actually having your own pony will help with that – you'll have to be focused and responsible; no more daydreaming! Now, I think you should get some rest, darling," she said, getting to her feet. "I think Dan has one last thing to say to you though." She turned to Dan. "Don't stay too long, will you? She's very tired."

"I won't, Mrs Black." Dan nodded as Georgia's mother, Melanie, Emma and Sophie filed out of

186

the room, leaving the two of them alone.

Georgia swallowed hard. Her palms were sticky. She didn't know why, but suddenly she felt a swirly feeling in the pit of her stomach as Dan turned towards her.

"You did amazing, Georgia Black, you know that?" he said as the door closed.

Georgia smiled weakly.

"And I've got something I wanted to ask you," he said in a soft, low voice.

Georgia looked puzzled.

"The midsummer dance is next week," he said, looking embarrassed. "I wondered … well … if you're better and all that. Well, would you, maybe, would you go with me?"

There was a moment's silence before Georgia nodded shyly.

"I take it that's a yes then?" Dan said.

"Yes," said Georgia. "Definitely!"

☆ ☆ ☆

It was a couple of days before Georgia was allowed to leave hospital, her wrist plastered in bright pink, the doctor's advice ringing in her ears. Georgia's mother picked her up with a delighted Pip sitting on the front seat of the car, thrilled to see her again.

"Can I go to the yard, Mum?" Georgia asked as soon she got in.

"Somehow I thought you might say that!" Lucy laughed. "I'm guessing that there's a certain pony you'd like to visit?"

Georgia hugged her mum, who turned the key in the ignition and swung the car out of the hospital car park. Soon they were driving slowly through the familiar lanes, flanked by thick green hedges laden with early blackberries.

As the car drove up the drive to Redgrove, Georgia could already see all the ponies. Lily was in her field, Callie was dozing beside her and Wilson was in the yard being groomed by Sophie, who smiled and waved as she got out of the car.

Georgia waved back, hurrying towards the paddock, desperate to see the little palomino. As soon as Lily caught sight of her, she whickered a greeting and trotted over to the fence.

Carefully, so as not to hurt her plastered wrist, Georgia let herself in through the gate and slung her good arm around the palomino's golden neck, closing her eyes and breathing in the little pony's heavenly scent. Lily was safe and, even better, she was hers! She might be just on loan but that was good enough for Georgia. She couldn't stop herself grinning from ear to ear.

Just then, Melanie came out of the house, the terriers yapping noisily at her heels. "She's looking really good considering what she's been through, isn't she?" She nodded in Lily's direction as she strolled over.

"She really is," Georgia agreed enthusiastically.

Sophie was still brushing out Wilson's tail as they walked back to the yard. She looked a bit sheepish and upset. "I just wanted to say how sorry I am," she said quietly.

"Why?" Georgia asked in surprise. "What for? It wasn't your fault!"

Sophie smiled sadly. "No, but Tory is – sorry, *was* – my friend. I should have realised what she was really like. She kept rushing off to meet this new boyfriend, and I was so mad at her, I just never listened to what she was actually saying. And all those questions she asked – I didn't realise she was using me to get inside info about Lily. I think she just wanted to impress that boy – he's older than her and stuff – and get in with the cool crowd who hang out at all the shows. Who are far cooler than me, apparently. Anyway, it backfired –

she's in loads of trouble now. I think her mother is going to ground her for life." The words came out in a rush.

"Tory has never been very nice to me," said Georgia, "but she's not totally bad either."

"I know," Sophie said. "But I'm going to try and pick my friends a bit more carefully from now on."

Georgia gave Sophie a big hug. She had always looked up to Sophie and thought she was pretty cool – popular and amazing at riding – but Georgia would hate to have been betrayed by someone she thought cared about her. She felt very lucky to have two such loyal best friends in Emma and Dan.

"Hey, you and Lily can come showing when your arm's better!" Sophie said brightly, changing the subject. "I think I'm going to concentrate on ponies for a while now – they are so much more reliable than people!"

Georgia laughed. "I'd love to start showing Lily, but I think there's a lot of work to do before we're at your standard. Still, you never know – one day!"

CHAPTER TWENTY-ONE

That day turned into one of the happiest of the whole of Georgia's summer holiday. She hung out with Sophie all day, watching her jump Wilson, and although she couldn't actually ride Lily because of her broken wrist, she put a lead rein on the palomino and had fun trotting her over a course of poles that they'd laid out in the paddock. Lily had such a lovely movement – bold and free, her tail held high and her hooves not even grazing one of the poles as she floated over them.

Georgia sighed. Life was pretty perfect.

As she led the little mare back into the yard for a rubdown, Em came rushing down the lane.

"You're not going to believe it, Georgia May!" she burbled. "Matt's just invited me to the midsummer dance!"

Georgia felt her heart lurch. The midsummer dance. It was this weekend!

"Matt?" Georgia puzzled. She couldn't think of anyone in their year with that name.

"You know, Matt Harris," she grinned. "From the year above."

Georgia smiled and raised her eyebrows.

"He's so cool, Georgia!" Emma gushed, her pretty face glowing. "I just don't know what to wear!"

Georgia just couldn't get as excited as her friend

over clothes. She hated dressing up and her hair hadn't been cut for ages. Still, in a strange sort of way, she was looking forward to the dance. She listened to Emma's plans for dresses and hair styles, and tried to be as enthusiastic as possible.

☆ ✪ ☆

On the evening of the midsummer dance, Georgia found herself sitting anxiously in the kitchen, trying to calm her nerves. Her mum had helped her get ready and she was waiting for Dan, who was due to come round at seven. Nervously, she played with a lock of hair.

"Georgia!" her mother chided. "Careful! It took me ages to do!"

"Sorry, Mum!" Georgia laughed. She had to admit her mother had done a great job of blow-drying it long and straight, before curling the ends. The summer sun had lightened it into a pale wheat blonde, and she had arranged a silver clip at the side that shimmered under the kitchen lights. Georgia actually felt pretty good, even if she was far happier in her T-shirt and jodhs.

Her mother had taken her shopping that morning to pick out a new dress, insisting she should choose whatever she wanted. Together they had decided on a light-pink dress that floated just above Georgia's knees, teaming it with a soft silver shawl. Finally she had chosen a pair of silver wedges, which she was admiring now, that set off her tanned feet and coral nail polish. The only blemish was the plaster on her wrist, but Mum had even decorated that with stick-on silver stars.

"Dan won't recognise you!" her mother said, smiling. "He's the luckiest boy in the school!"

"Mum!" Georgia exclaimed as the doorbell rang. "We're just friends!"

Dan – apparently feeling as awkward as Georgia,

but looking good in his dinner jacket and bow tie – was waiting on the doorstep. Georgia smiled shyly at him.

"You look really nice, Georgia!" he said, breaking into a grin.

"Thanks, so do you," Georgia whispered back.

Mrs Black dropped them off at the dance, which was being held in the school grounds. There was a marquee decorated with gold balloons and fairy lights, a flashing dance floor and, to Georgia's delight, a chocolate fountain and a delicious-looking buffet!

Emma came rushing up the minute she saw them, with her date in tow. She was grinning from ear to ear. "Isn't this the coolest, Georgia!" she said excitedly.

"I guess," said Georgia.

Emma looked lovely in a bright-yellow dress. She waved her white beaded bag about enthusiastically. "Come on! We have to dance!" she exclaimed.

She whirled Georgia off to the dance floor with Matt and Dan following behind. The whole school was there, it seemed, and Georgia was immediately surrounded by her friends, all curious to know why her wrist was in plaster. Then she became caught up in the music – she'd never realised dancing could be so much fun before!

Finally, when she couldn't dance any longer, she collapsed on the lawn outside with Dan and they shared a plate of canapés. The evening was warm, and the night sky enveloped Georgia as softly as the silver shawl slung loosely around her shoulders. After giggling for a while at the sight of their teachers hitting the dance floor, Dan turned to Georgia.

"You know, this has been the best summer ever," he murmured.

Georgia looked into his eyes. How had she never noticed they were so blue? Like the palest cornflower. She felt her heart tremble as Dan went on.

"It hasn't been easy after my mum ... well, you know," he said. "Meeting you, and Em, and Lily, and Melanie and the horses, has really cheered me up. I love spending time with you all, but especially you, Georgia." He smiled at her gently. Georgia felt the wind rushing in her ears as she blushed and lowered her eyes.

When she dared look up at Dan, he was still grinning at her. He nudged her gently in the ribs, and laughed. "Even if you are totally pony mad!" he said.

The two of them burst out laughing. "That may be so, Dan," Georgia replied, "but I think you love the ponies just as much as I do now!"

"You may be right!" Dan nodded. Before

Georgia could say anything else, he jumped to his feet and pulled her up by her good hand. "Come on," he said. "Let's show those teachers how to dance!"

☆ ☆ ☆

Despite the late night, Georgia was still up at Redgrove bright and early the next morning. There wasn't much left of the summer holidays now, and she wanted to make the most of every single moment she had with Lily. She had decided to take her for a walk on the lead rein and show her some of the scenery of the surrounding area.

The beautiful palomino really seemed to be enjoying herself. She was relaxed and calm, her lovely ears pricked forwards, drinking in the new sights as they ambled up the path at the back of Redgrove.

Stopping her at the brow of the hill, Georgia sighed with pleasure. She'd had such a great time

the previous evening with Dan and Em and all her other friends – she was so lucky. And to top it all, she now had her dream pony. This summer had turned out to be better than she could have ever imagined.

Georgia fondly patted Lily's golden neck and then leaned in to whisper her thanks to the little pony. She stood back and smiled. Just being with Lily was enough, but as soon as her wrist was healed they would have so much fun riding out together and maybe one day even training to compete.

Lily had been at Redgrove for such a short time but already it felt as though the beautiful palomino belonged there with Georgia. The two of them, together. What could be better than that?

ACKNOWLEDGEMENTS

Nosy Crow would like to thank Katy Marriott Payne for letting her lovely Palomino pony star on the covers of this series.